WALTER

WALTER

Ashley Sievwright

Clouds of Magellan | Melbourne

First published 2012
Clouds of Magellan, Melbourne, Australia
www.cloudsofmagellan.net

ISBN: 978-0-9874037-0-4

WITH THANKS TO
Eleonora, Gordon and Amanda

CONTENTS

1.
DON'T GET ON THE NEXT TRAIN

Walter felt a raindrop on his cheek. He put his hand out and looked up at the sky. In the east the sky was blue and the early morning sun was lazily low and heavy on the horizon, the colour of an early morning wee. But directly above was a dark cloud which was now (yes, another drop, and then another fell on his hand) raining on the suburb of Wintergardens. It rained upon the umbrellas of the early morning commuters who were on their way to the train station; upon the windscreens of the cars backing out of driveways and making their way to the on-ramp of the nearby freeway; upon the roofs of the houses which were bright orange in the wet sunlight; upon the grass and other foliage which was virulent green, sleek and wet, as if it was visibly, palpably photosynthesising before his eyes. The raindrops themselves were picked out mid-flight by the sun, like chipped diamonds—they looked as if they would hurt, but of course they didn't. Everything looked shiny bright and new, as if the entire suburb was fresh out of the automatic car-wash.

Walter rolled his eyes and made a dismissive sound with his tongue. *Sun-showers.* This wasn't weather, he thought, as he walked through the rain towards the train station, this was somewhere in between weather, unreal and undecided and totally, what was the word? Yes that was it—*totally unconvincing.*

It didn't seem to him an odd opinion to have. He didn't wonder how it was he remained unconvinced about something that actually existed, something real and tangible that he was walking through.

Of course he knew it was real. He could feel the sun on his face and the raindrops on the back of his hand. These were fact—hard meteorological fact. This was weather. It was happening. But these facts, he felt, still didn't make it aesthetically convincing. He actually said the words in his head, *aesthetically unconvincing*.

Walter often had his own internal monologues going on. Not voices inside his head as such, not other people or entities talking to him or telling him to do things, nothing like that, nothing *crazy*. Just a running monologue of his own voice, his own thoughts, in his head—himself, inside, looking at things, considering, summing up, sorting, categorising, commenting, pigeon-holing, judging and critiquing the world around him. Walter was a pedant, a fiend for accuracy, for boiled-down pithiness, and it made him feel good to find the right words, the right way to express himself, even if it was only in his head. But everyone had that, didn't they? It was called thinking wasn't it? *Everyone thinks*, Walter thought to himself.

OK, so his internal monologues weren't always only internal. Sometimes he would say something out loud, sure, talk to himself. Everyone did that too, didn't they, on occasion? On the road, for example, in the car by himself, he would say things out loud, as if speaking to other drivers—criticise their driving, or point out their mistakes, or just rant at them, call them names. One time he lost his temper with a slow driver in front of him in the fast lane of the freeway and he came out with: *do you have to drive like such a pussy?* This so amused him at the time, the fact that he had described someone as a pussy—what was he, ten years old?—that he couldn't help laughing at himself. He then said: *pussy-driver* over and over again, enjoying the sound of it, the silliness of it. He even did it in different accents, starting with a BBC announcer kind of voice, and ending up as Samuel L Jackson.

He wasn't really a swearing kind of person, and as a result he came out with the strangest things, co-opting as his own a whole heap of slightly inappropriate (for him) catch-phrases or insults he had gleaned from television or books, magazines, film-clips shown on early morning weekend television, and all of them, without a doubt every single one of them, sounded foreign coming out of his middle-class, conventional mouth. This was the other side of the well-spoken pedant, the Walter who could call someone a pussy-driver.

Sometimes his internal voice might rehearse conversations he would have, if he could ever work up the courage, with his Supervisor (a young Indian man called Devadarshan or Dev for short—a 'youth' Walter called him, fifteen years his junior). Things he might say to his wife Maggie (but you didn't, as a rule, say things to Maggie). Or he might practice what he was going to talk about at his next appointment with Dr Feldman (his psychiatrist—but again, no, he wasn't crazy).

If anyone ever noticed him, ever saw him snigger to himself as he made a joke in his head, or make an odd facial expression as if coming to a conclusion, or if they heard him in his car, calling out strange adolescent insults at other drivers, then, yes, they might not be quite so sure that this was all normal and there was nothing-to-see-here. They might, as a matter of fact, suspect, just quietly, that Walter was a bit of a kook.

His full name was Walter Kovak. It was, perhaps, an old-fashioned first name for a man of only forty-two years of age, but his parents, Poles who had immigrated to Australia in the 1950s, had named him after his grandfather, whose name had actually been Waclaw, the Polish for Walter. He was thankful he hadn't been lumbered with Waclaw. His parents had been quite old when he was born, a late and unplanned baby, and both had since passed away.

There were traces of his Polish ancestry in Walter's face. He had a heavy jaw and a wide forehead. He had a strong rather big nose, well-shaped lips and big, watery eyes. His hair grew dark and thick and square across his forehead—he combed it to the back and generally parted it on the right side although it never stayed. His skin was quite pale and pasty, and if he did get sun he would usually turn pink, sometimes burn and peel without turning brown.

He was of medium height and regularly proportioned, thick-set without being overweight. He was hairless on his chest and arms, but as hairy as a goat around his privates and on his legs—well perhaps not as hairy as a goat, but almost, although this wasn't perhaps as immediately obvious to the general observer. He had collapsed arches, so purchased running shoes specifically designed to support his feet and inner soles for his other shoes—as a result when he walked he walked correctly, on the outside edge of his feet, down onto the balls of his feet and off the toe. Aware of a propensity for lower back pain, at work he sat stolidly with legs slightly apart, bent at the knee, his feet flat on the floor, his back straight. In general, there was no sway in his hips, no swing in his gait, no rhythm in him at all it seemed. Walter was essentially ergonomically correct.

Mick, a workmate of Walter's, a young man who regularly slumped casually at his desk, often slipping right down in his chair, just clinging on to the seat with the bones in his bum, and who would have rocked backwards on it had it not been on wheels, said of Walter:

'There he goes, sweeping the floor again.' He meant, so he explained to a workmate, that the way Walter walked it looked as if he had a broomstick up his arse—unfair, perhaps, but also accurate.

Walter worked in the city, at an insurance firm, and he travelled to work every day on the 7.15am train from Wintergardens, an express train into the city and through the Melbourne City Loop, and got off the train at Flagstaff.

During the working week Walter wore the accepted corporate attire, but there was something slightly not quite right about that too. The suits he wore, invariably navy or grey, but never quite the right navy or grey, were not well-fitted and were shiny around the seams, firstly from being cheap and secondly from being dry-cleaned too often. His ties were cheap and lumpy. His shoes, black, designed for comfort rather than looks, were thick-soled and chunky. His socks were the sort with strategically placed elastic so that they stayed up—All Day Socks, they were called, and he had monitored this the first day he'd worn them, out of curiosity, to see if at any point he had to pull up his socks. He had not.

The above is a comprehensive description of Walter, but it must be said that no-one, not a single person, noticed each and every one of these things about Walter. Certainly some people noticed one or two things, but no-one noticed all of them, because there was something else about Walter, perhaps the most important aspect of him. He was completely inconsequential. Inconsequentiality covered him like an invisible lacquer. He was the sort of person you would look through rather than at, the type you would pass by in the street without noticing, the type you could see time and time again in the lift at work without actually knowing what he did or what his name was and think: *Does he work for us?*

He was the type to be overlooked by waiters and shopkeepers. Over the years so many service-people had either taken so long to notice him, or ignored him altogether, that he had developed quite a thing about it. It had got to the point where he expected to be ignored. Moreover, he seemed sometimes even to will it upon himself. Where a raised hand and an 'excuse me' might have worked wonders, Walter would instead sit there, or stand there, quietly, waiting his turn, and in his head he'd be telling himself that they weren't going to see him or say anything to him or serve him, and he would be counting the moments of this affront, this indignity, this injustice, on an imaginary stopwatch in his head, thinking: *typical—bloody typical!* And if it went on long enough he might stalk out of the shop or restaurant or wherever it was on the balls of his feet, and tell himself in a stern voice inside his head that he would never to go back there. They may never know it, whoever they were, whichever business had shunned him, but they were from that moment on denied his custom, which over the years may have added up to a significant amount of income. This was how he made a stand, such as it was.

When Walter arrived at the city bound platform of Wintergardens station the sky was still grey and clouded over, but the rain had stopped, the sun-shower was over. He put his umbrella down and tapped it on the ground a couple of times to clear it of moisture.

The men and women surrounding Walter on the train station were mostly the same type as him, in that they were dressed in the rather lazy version of corporate wear that passed muster for the majority in Melbourne, but otherwise, Walter felt, the only thing he had in common with his fellow commuters was that they all lived in Wintergardens. Just like other manufactured suburbs on the outskirts of Melbourne and other Australian cities, Wintergardens had not had time to establish a personality of its own—or, perhaps more accurately, it had multiple personalities but none of them had so far exerted themselves as dominant.

People had come to Wintergardens mostly for the same reason—the house and land packages were, if not cheap, then at least quite affordable. So there were young families making a start with their first home, unable to afford anything in an inner city suburb where prices for even the most basic of townhouses or units had skyrocketed. There were retirees who had perhaps found that their superannuation was not as much as they hoped for or needed. And there were a high ratio of immigrant families, mostly from the African and Arab nations which seemed, Walter thought, to be where most of the immigrant traffic came from these days. And India, he amended in his head, thinking of Dev.

This multiple personality was beginning to make itself felt visually up and down the streets of Wintergardens. Most properties were treated with the utmost care and respect, with neat little gardens, carefully cleaned windows and bleached white stone between twin concrete strips of the driveway, but gradually there emerged a house here and there with overgrown lawns, two or three cars in the driveway, and smeared windows with the curtains all bunched up because of furniture pushed against them from inside.

Walter noticed two Somali men who lived just around the corner from him in one such house. Brothers he thought, with skin as black as his own nugget-polished shoes. They were very tall and incredibly lean, with shiny suits in dark blue and deep purple, worn very loose-fitting. A woman a little way away from them wore a full veil covering her hair, neatly pinned with multiple hair pins. She also wore a fashionable woollen skirt and jacket cut so close-fitting as to be eye-popping. There were people from many other cultures on the platform, but who could tell anymore what they were or where they were from, Walter thought? Unless they were fresh off the boat it was sometimes difficult to tell. Either they were from mixed parentage, or they were second generation immigrants (like Walter himself), or they were first generation but totally homogenised in some way. That was what Australia was now, Walter felt, a hodge-podge of different cultures adding up to a cultural non-identity. Not that he was racist, he would have said—which is what everyone who is a little bit racist does say.

The truth is that Walter, with his back straight and his chin up, his eye fixed on some vague spot in the middle distance, exuding an air of superiority and disapproval, not about anything in particular, was, without knowing it, out of place in his own suburb. He was, essentially, white bread—middle class, second generation immigrant Australian. Not that there weren't others like him, there were, and they tended to stick together; but they didn't notice that in a suburb like Wintergardens they were not in the majority.

Walter had probably seen most of his fellow commuters on other weekday mornings at approximately the same time at this train station, but he was not familiar enough with any of them to be on speaking terms. He was not the sort of person to be over-familiar with work colleagues or speak to strangers on the street or at the train station. So it was a bit of a surprise to him when one of his fellow commuters spoke to him that morning—a man, standing just next to him on the platform.

'I think the rain's going to hold off for a while,' said the man, looking up at the clouds.

'Just a sun-shower,' Walter said amiably. Then he raised his left arm and jerked his arm forward to bring his watch out from his shirt cuff. His watch showed 7.14am exactly. He turned and looked down the tracks for an oncoming train—there wasn't one.

The man next to him made a clicking noise with his tongue.

'Late again,' he said.

Walter made a non-committal sound, but said nothing.

'It's good for the garden at least,' said the man.

'Yes,' Walter agreed. *Save me*, he thought, *from these boring pleasantries.* He looked down the tracks again and this time saw that the train was approaching.

It was then that Walter's fellow commuter, from behind him, said something else, something Walter wasn't quite sure he heard properly. He spun around and looked at the man directly, looked at him properly for the first time—an older man, grey-haired, with crow's feet by his eyes, but an otherwise unlined face, grey suit, white shirt, red tie, briefcase. He had a mild, ordinary kind of face, and blank, light-blue eyes. Like Walter he didn't seem to fit. He should have been at a train station on the other side of town, in one of those leafy middle-to-outer suburbs. He wasn't looking at Walter, he was looking towards the approaching train.

'What was that?' Walter asked. 'What did you just say?'

The man looked at him with a polite smile.

'I beg your pardon?' he asked.

'What did you say? Just then? About the train?'

'About the train?'

'This train.'

'I'm sorry, I'm not sure what you mean.' The man smiled again, but not as politely, not genuinely. He gently but firmly shook his head, signifying that as far as he was concerned the conversation was at an end.

Walter had heard correctly. He knew he had. His hearing was perfect. The man beside him on the platform had said to him, quite close and clear behind him, as if he'd even leaned in a bit closer to say it:

Don't get on the next train.

The train pulled into the station and the displaced air rushed over the platform and through the waiting commuters. When it had stopped completely they began to shuffle forward and into the carriage. Walter unconsciously took a step towards the carriage along with them, alongside the man who had spoken to him. He was going to say something to him, but before he could the man stepped inside the carriage and was lost to Walter amid the other commuters. Walter stepped forward to follow him, but hesitated, stopped. He was suddenly aware of the dampness in his shoes and trouser cuffs from walking through the rain, an uncomfortable dampness that made his leg hairs stand against his trousers.

After a moment he realised that he was the only person left on the platform. Everyone else had entered the train, but he remained rooted to the spot, just a step away from the open carriage door, his feet planted firmly in his comfortably soled shoes, his upper body moving slightly forward and backwards, like a praying mantis on a twig.

A couple of people from within the carriage noticed him, hesitating as he was, and their eyes focussed, they looked at him. Walter felt a flush of embarrassment mount in his cheeks as another and another of the people in the train carriage noticed his mantis-like hesitation, met his eye and became, as one, slightly wary, as if thinking: *Why is this man not getting on the train? Why is he behaving in this unexpected way?* And then finally: *He isn't going to delay the train is he?*

But he couldn't move. He couldn't move.

Then, hovering, stuck as he was in the middle of such a horrible social *faux pas*, a terrible breach of train etiquette, the moment was broken by the beeping warning from the train that the doors were about to close. He stepped backwards, gingerly, away from the train, back behind the yellow line. The doors closed, the train slowly pulled away from the station and the carriage-full of people looking at him was borne away. He was alone on the completely empty platform and the moment was over.

He closed his eyes.

Don't get on the next train.

But why had the man said such a thing? As a warning? Against what? What possible reason could there be for such a warning? What possible danger could there be to him, Walter, if he had boarded that train? His rational mind, and he was a very rational man, rebelled against the very idea of what had just happened to him—and yet there it was, the man had warned him not to board the train and as a result he had not boarded the train.

Walter felt annoyed with himself, foolish, edgy and agitated. It was a familiar feeling. Well, not as familiar lately, but still familiar. However, with a concerted effort and a deep-breathing technique he had learned from Dr Feldman, Walter attempted to put aside the feeling.

Imagine your fear, he told himself in his head. *Do you see it?*

'Yes.' He nodded.

Would you like to get rid of it?

'Yes.' He nodded.

Then imagine screwing it up into a little ball.

His right hand made a fist.

And throwing it away.

His right hand made a somewhat muted throwing gesture.

It never worked, not really, but as he opened his eyes he was aware, not that he had got rid of his fear, but that he had mastered it, had forced it back down and snibbed the lid closed on it, and that was enough to be getting on with.

2.
ON THE JOB AT EQUITY

He ended up driving his car to work that day. At first he was going to catch the next train and he stood waiting on the platform as more corporate commuters turned up to wait alongside him. But as the minutes ticked by he felt increasingly positive that he wasn't going to get on the next train either, so he returned through the still-wet streets of Wintergardens to his house, got the car out and headed off towards the freeway on-ramp where he queued with all the other cars.

It wasn't, as it turned out, a great decision. He ended up caught in a bumper-to-bumper traffic jam on the West Gate Bridge where there was one lane out due to a broken down truck. The clouds had disappeared completely by this stage and the sun was further up in the sky, warming the wet bridge until it seemed to be steaming. Walter had the windows up and the air-con on low. He also had a CD playing. He was, perhaps incongruously, listening to a chill-out album called Ibiza Summer, with slow beats, the sound of waves crashing on a shore and a man's voice chanting abstract and vaguely sexual lyrics. *Yeah baby, oooh, yeah baby.*

Walter's mobile phone, secure in its hands-free cradle, rang. He glanced at the display and saw who was calling.

Oh crap! Maggie!

His wife's actual name was Margaret but she was only ever called Maggie, and the words 'oh crap', at least in Walter's head, were often aligned with her name.

Walter had been fascinated by Maggie when he was a young man, absolutely fascinated, and had married her presuming blithely that theirs would be a happy marriage. The best that could be said of it now was that it wasn't actively unhappy.

She was an attractive woman, with dark hair, pearly skin and a sense of entitlement about her. She had grown up having her mother, Arlette, tell her she was a princess, could do anything she wanted in life, have anything she wanted. A sense of entitlement was perhaps not an attractive trait, and on Maggie who was a little aloof and withdrawn, it was sometimes unattractive.

Arlette had been, albeit very briefly, a model—one of those Paris End of Collins Street set who were incredibly chic there for a few years in the fifties. To this day she had on display the photo Helmet Newton had taken of her in a stiff shift coat, holding a square handbag and (apparently) hailing a cab, very po-faced and straight-armed, with one leg kicked out behind her.

Following her short modelling career, in which Paton pattern books featured heavily, Arlette worked for a number of years, until her marriage and Maggie's subsequent birth, as a consultant with a finishing school. Even in the mid to late 60s the idea of a finishing school in Melbourne was anachronistic, but it had survived to the present day. It was now called the Potter-Hopkins School of Personal Development, but it still ran short courses in manners, grooming, which cutlery to use at dinner, and how to get out of a car without showing your undies.

Walter was not a fan of his mother-in-law. She was pinched and thin, dressed in power suits from the 80s, which now stood off her thin frame like dolls' clothes. She wore bright patches of rouge and lipstick and her hair was thin and brittle, tortured regularly by permanent wave and blow-waved in a big curve off her face every morning. She looked, he thought, like a voodoo doll of herself.

There was (Walter would have said, 'unfortunately') a little bit of Arlette in Maggie. A little bit. It was in the way she moved and the way she held her cigarette—yes she smoked, Walter could not get her to quit. It was in the way she ate. It was in the way she got out of a car without showing her undies.

Maggie had told Walter early on in their relationship, and it was one of the things about her which fascinated him, that she had worn white gloves in public until the age of twelve.

He was mostly unsure about what was going on under his wife's careful exterior. Sometimes he was wary of her, and other times he was, well, not to put too fine a point on it, just a little scared of her. With good reason it would seem, as just the other night she had tried to smother him in his sleep. Although when he said it like that, said it actually to Maggie: 'I can't believe you tried to smother me in my sleep,' she just scoffed and repeated: 'Smother you,' in a mocking voice, as if he was just being a very silly boy. But what else did you call it when someone put a pillow over your face while you were asleep?

'You were having a nightmare,' Maggie said blandly.

'That's no … reason to put a pillow …' He was panting.

Maggie closed her eyes.

'Do you think you could move to the spare room? I really need to get some sleep.'

'Well, yes. I suppose … but there was no need for … that.'

OK, so he had been having one of his nightmares. They had been a regular feature of their lives over the past year, since his return from hospital, but for some time now they hadn't been as bad. He still had them occasionally, and he knew that it must be annoying for Maggie, being woken up like that in the middle of the night by a jittery, flailing person—because that's what she'd described him as, jittery and flailing, not a description he relished, not exactly the way a kind, supportive, considerate wife might describe her husband at one of his more vulnerable moments.

He and Maggie had been married nearly fifteen years. What did you get for that anniversary he wondered? His more blokey neighbours, he felt sure, would be certain to answer: 'Parole.' Parole, Walter thought, mightn't be a bad thing, because no matter which way you cut it, you had to consider that your marriage had got to a pretty bad place when your wife was putting a pillow over your face in the middle of the night.

Despite the rather large number of things that Walter's internal voice had imagined saying to his wife, or he'd told Dr Feldman he would like to say to his wife, as he pressed the button on his mobile phone that morning in his car, stuck in traffic on the West Gate Bridge, muting the chill-out music and answering the phone simultaneously, he had no intention of saying any of them.

'Hiya,' he answered. Very un-him.

'Why did you take the car?' Maggie said. No preamble. Not really a question.

'I missed the train. I was running late. I needed to get in to work in a hurry.' The irony of the traffic being at that moment at a complete standstill was not lost on Walter. He looked at the time on the dash display. He was late.

'But I need the car today, Walter.'

She had her own car, their second car, a little blue Mazda, but it was at the shop after 'a little bingle' as Maggie had described it.

'I'm sorry. I really am sorry, but it was just that …'

'Oh never mind.' There was a beep and the call was terminated. Maggie was usually the one to terminate the call.

Walter pressed the End Call button on the phone viciously and said in a falsely cheery voice: 'Bye then.' A car behind him beeped its horn. He looked up and noticed that the traffic had moved forward about ten metres and stopped again.

'OK OK!' Walter said to the car in his rear-view mirror.

He took his foot from the brake and rolled forward. The car behind stuck closely to his bumper, moving forward with small jerks. Walter didn't like tailgaters. Then again who did? He gently applied the brakes and rolled ever so slowly to a stop a good couple of car-lengths away from the car in front of him. He glanced in the rear-view mirror again with a slight smirk on his face.

'Arse-wipe,' he said.

*

When Walter finally got into the city it was already 8.45am and he was a good forty-five minutes late. This didn't matter particularly as most of the others in the office didn't start until 9.00am, but he liked to begin earlier. That first hour in the morning, with the rest of the office half deserted, was the most productive part of the day. He got most of his work done then. The remainder of the day was fragmented and disjointed by the comings and goings of the rest of the office staff. The simplest of tasks were interrupted and lengthened, he felt, by phone calls, or people turning up and wanting to speak to him face to face. Of course this was partly because of that most horrible of arrangements: open plan.

He entered the car park and resigned himself to the long drive up and around the levels to the top. By this time of the morning all the lower levels were full. In fact he had to drive all the way up to the very top level before he found a spot. He pulled in and turned off the engine but not the music. For a moment he sat there in his climate controlled interior, in his own world, a world without tailgate drivers and open plan offices, a world possibly without Maggie, certainly without her nagging, and definitely without trains. But perhaps that was asking a bit too much of Ibiza Summer. He turned off the music and got out of the car.

*

Walter worked for Equity Insurance. Their motto, as displayed under the logo was 'Probity, Honesty, Integrity'. He had always found this motto a little embarrassing—what were they, Knights of the Round Table? He wished he had been in the boardroom with the senior executive team around a table the day they were brainstorming virtues appropriate for the motto, so that he could have thrown something a bit more interesting into the mix—

chastity perhaps, or even sobriety? Cleanliness? Everyone knew that was right up there next to godliness.

The Equity Insurance firm had offices in William Street in the Melbourne CBD. That part of town was resolutely corporate, a hive of activity during the working week, but mostly dead in the evenings and during the weekends, apart from the nearby King Street with its lap-dancing venues and grotty reputation. The Equity Insurance building wasn't a particularly interesting building. It was built somewhere in the late 80s and there was a huge echoing foyer lined with white faux-granite and mirrors, two huge revolving doors at the front and a bank of six lifts. There were twenty-three floors, a number of them given over to various areas of Equity Insurance—financial services, life insurance, wealth management, the executive floor and HR. The call centres were elsewhere, although not yet offshore, Walter was pleased to note.

Walter worked in life insurance as an actuarial analyst. It wasn't a particularly interesting job, but he was a numbers man, he was a spreadsheet kind of guy and so it suited him. Given his age, he should probably have risen naturally up the ladder a little higher than he had, but just as waiters and shopkeepers overlooked him, so did the executive team when it came to promotion, new opportunities, project work, and so on. In this case though, Walter was more or less happy to remain 'under the radar' (horrid term) because in common, he was sure, with much of the population and certainly many of his co-workers, he didn't really give a stuff about his job. Well, he did and he didn't. It suited him, certainly, considering he had an aptitude for the sort of number crunching required and didn't particularly feel interested in, or good at, interacting with the public in the form of Equity Insurance clients. The wage suited him, which was good without being incredible and was paid into his account fortnightly, the four weeks of holiday suited him, taken pretty much when he liked, and the options for voluntary contributions to his Super and car payments suited him, reducing his wage below a certain threshold which meant he got taxed less. The routine of it suited him, and the longer he was there, the more he knew the work, the less it impinged on him, the less he had to think about it. It was this more than anything that suited him, the ease of it all. In a way he no longer even noticed that he worked for Equity Insurance.

Sometimes he wondered, sometimes, in a flash of perspective, for just a second, he wondered what he was saving himself for, but that thought flustered him a little, in some way he didn't understand. It was one of those thoughts with a huge unexplored well of blackness behind it, and it wasn't really in Walter's nature to plumb those depths.

His team leader, Dev, a self-described 'young gun', was straight out of university into Equity, and had already had two promotions. He was snippy about punctuality, but luckily so was Walter, so that was never a bone of contention. Even so there was little love lost between them. Walter didn't have a very good relationship with any of his co-workers really, probably because he wasn't the type to go out to the pub with his workmates, or for a curry with Dev. In fact, in his last performance appraisal (a demeaning experience having his performance appraised by Dev) one of the comments made was: '… needs to be a better team player'. Walter had smiled at Dev benignly during this part of the performance appraisal process, but in his head he was thinking: *team player this*, and imagined himself giving Dev two middle fingers.

A while back Walter had told Dr Feldman that he longed sometimes to tell Dev to *go get fucked*. Those specific three words, he thought, although not grammatically stellar, were important—not only was Dev to *get fucked*, which was, of course, quite damning in itself, but he was to *go* to do it, go, that is, away from him, Walter, and do it somewhere out of his sight, because he couldn't even be bothered watching it—those three words, he felt, so perfectly expressed disinterest and disdain in equal measures, he was quite pleased with them.

'So this Dev makes you feel angry?' Dr Feldman had asked him.

'Angry?' Walter had repeated, wide eyed.

'Yes. You sounded very angry just then. When you said you wanted to tell him to go get fucked. I mean, that sounded angry to me.'

'Did it?'

'U-huh.'

'Oh,' Walter had said to the doctor. 'I do apologise.'

'Why don't you tell him how you feel?'

'Tell him?'

'Yes. Not perhaps in those exact words ...'

'Oh,' Walter said, slightly flustered. 'I couldn't do that. He's Indian.'

*

Walter had a cubicle in an open plan office. His was a very neat desk with computer, phone and various stationery items arranged neatly, parallel to each other, all tidy and rigidly spaced, as if measured. He didn't know it, but sometimes while he was away from his desk, out to lunch or in a meeting or something, his co-worker Mick would come up to his desk and move one of the items, maybe his stapler, so that it sat cocked a little to the side, just the smallest bit out of alignment. Then, when Walter returned to his desk, Mick, and sometimes some of the others, would be watching from a few cubicles away, peeking over the carpet divider, waiting for Walter to notice and correct the position of the stapler, which he did immediately, automatically, every time. He didn't hear their titters of laughter, or if he did he presumed they were laughing at something else.

That morning was exactly the same as any other in Walter's work life—that was kind of the point with him—but in the back of his mind he was unable to stop thinking about that man at the station. *Don't get on the next train.* It was there with him all morning, like something hovering over his shoulder, in his peripheral vision. By mid-morning he decided he had to do something about it. He went and got himself a cup of tea—first things first—black with two sugars. Then, after checking the whereabouts of Dev, whose cubicle backed onto his (he was safely ensconced in the Senior Staff Meeting and wouldn't be out until lunch) he logged on to the internet and checked a couple of local news websites. He glanced down through the headlines—something about the outcome of a major crime trial, sporting news, some political mumbo-jumbo about the next budget, blah blah, but nothing was reported as having occurred on or to the 7.15am express from Wintergardens to the city. Perhaps it was ridiculous of him to think that something had happened, but checking the internet news pages, finding out, knowing for sure, that wasn't ridiculous at all, that was just conscientious.

Perhaps the story, whatever it might be, just hadn't been reported yet. It was only—he glanced at the time on the bottom right hand side of his computer screen—10.45am after all. He tapped his fingers on his desk, then, after a moment, he looked around the office. Most of the desks near his were empty. The coast, as they say, was clear.

He typed another web address in the browser and found the website of the company that ran the suburban train system in Melbourne. A few more clicks and he had found a phone number for enquiries. He picked up his phone, dialled zero for an outside line, then dialled the number.

The call was answered by a recorded voice giving Walter various options. He pressed zero to be put through to a real person. Soon enough someone answered. A woman.

'Hello,' Walter said. 'I wonder if you could put me through to …' Only then did he realise that he probably should have thought ahead to this moment. 'Information,' he finished lamely.

'Information on our services, Sir?'

'Well no, not that. Information about …'

'Timetables?'

'No, no. Is there someone I could talk to who could tell me about the … well, tell me if anything happened to the 7.15am express from Wintergardens this morning?'

'Tell you if anything happened to it?'

'That's right.'

'Like what, Sir?'

'I don't know. An accident? A … something. I don't know.'

There was a considerable pause before the voice resumed.

'Could you please hold the line, Sir? I'll get someone to speak with you.'

Walter waited. He swapped the phone to his other ear and gave a quick look around the office. No-one close enough to overhear.

Soon a new voice was on the phone. A man this time.

'Hello, Sir. Is there something I can help you with?'

'I just wanted to know if anything happened to the Wintergardens train this morning.'

'Could I have your name, please, Sir?'

Walter hesitated. He blinked a couple of times. *Oh crap!*

He hung up quickly, slamming the phone down with such violence that a conversation a couple of cubicles away stopped dead. He sat hunched and still until the conversation started up again.

His hand was still on the phone when it rang. He jumped and withdrew his hand to his chest as if it was burnt. Then, after a moment and a breath or two, he picked it up again. It was Ros-at-Reception (he thought of her like that, not Ros, but Ros-at-Reception), a middle-aged woman who had obviously once been told, possibly on some professional development course, that she should always answer the phone with a smile because the person on the other end could hear it. Having done the job perhaps a little too long, the smile had gradually become a grimace, and her voice, when she answered the phone, 'Equity-Insurance-good-afternoon', sounded lilting, arch and incredibly insincere.

'Man here to see you,' she said shortly. She didn't smile for internal calls.

'Really?' Walter didn't usually get visitors to the office. 'Who is it?'

There was a pause as Ros-at-Reception presumably asked the visitor for a name.

'A Mr Michael Everaardt,' she said.

Walter had never heard the name before. Didn't have a clue who it was.

'I'll come round.'

The man waiting in Reception was young, dressed in denim jeans and an untucked button shirt, with a sports jacket over it. He had brown hair and a triangular tuft of facial hair under his bottom lip. He was slightly crumpled and gave Walter the impression of being a slacker. He extended his hand as Walter approached, and Walter, still not knowing who he was or what this was about, extended his own hand. They shook hands, three pumps, up and down, of medium firmness—entirely appropriate for a greeting in a business setting.

'Mr Kovak?' the young man asked.

'That's right. And you're Michael … Everaardt was it?'

'That's right.'

'What can I do for you?'

'I wonder if I can have a minute or two of your time?' he said, not really explaining anything.

Selling something, Walter wondered? Although that didn't seem right.

'I suppose so,' he said. He checked with Ros-at-Reception that the smaller of the meeting rooms just off Reception was free and they went in there. He indicated a seat and the young man sat down, folded his hands on the table and leaned toward Walter.

Not selling something, Walter decided. The body language was wrong. He had recently done some reading on body language. This man was trying to ingratiate himself, certainly, but not in a sales kind of way. This was something else.

Walter's mind flashed back to the phone call he had made to the train company just moments ago, and flushed with embarrassment and guilt. How stupid to ring a transport company and ask if anything had happened to one of their services. He remembered how the person who he had been transferred to, the one who kept calling him Sir, had asked him for his name, and how he had then hung up. He couldn't have sounded any more like a terrorist if he tried.

He looked at the young man sitting with his hands folded on the table. Surely they couldn't have traced him so quickly.

'I want to talk to you about the accident,' the young man said.

*

'Tell me about the accident,' Dr Feldman had said.

'Why?' Walter had responded in a surly manner.

This was in the early days, soon after coming out of hospital, before he had got into his groove with Dr Feldman.

'I want you to.'

'Why? I don't understand why.'

'I'm asking you to, that's why.'

'You know what happened.'

'Correct.'

'So why do you want me to tell you? It's stupid. It's irrelevant. It's unnecessary.'

'All of those things, yes. But Walter, that's why you're here.'

Yeah yeah. He was there to talk about the accident. The Australian Centre for Post Traumatic Mental Health had referred him to Dr Feldman. That's where all this psychiatrist stuff had started. But he didn't want to talk about the accident—he didn't even want to think about it.

*

Michael Everaardt sat watching Walter who seemed a million miles away, his eyes blank and staring straight ahead.

'Are you OK?' he asked after a while.

He touched Walter on the elbow.

At the touch Walter's eyes slowly focussed.

'Can I get you something? Some water?' Michael asked.

'No …' Walter said. 'No thanks. Who are you?'

Michael wriggled in his chair. This, he knew, was where things were going to get sticky—stickier.

'I'm a writer.'

'Oh,' Walter said with considerable dislike. 'You mean a journalist, don't you?'

'I know you feel you were hounded by the press, but if you could just give me just a few minutes … I can assure you, you'll have final say on what's in and what's …'

Walter didn't appear to be listening. He got up slowly from his chair and stood with his feet firmly planted. Michael didn't know this about Walter, of course, having never met him, but the stolid, sturdy stance was very much a Walter thing.

'No,' he said simply.

Michael stood also and put his hand out to touch Walter on the arm soothingly.

'I'm sure we could come to some …'

'No we couldn't,' Walter said, moving away slightly. 'I think you should go.'

So he went. There was little else he could do. Coming as he had without making an appointment, without announcing his intentions or his profession, was stupid enough, without compounding the felony by making a complete arsehole of himself now.

Michael considered himself a pragmatic kind of guy and, with only the slightest head-nod of acknowledgement to Walter, he walked back out into the foyer and pressed the lift-call button.

As amazing as it was considering their shared circumstances, this had been his very first face-to-face meeting with Walter Kovak. He had seen the wife before, Maggie was it? But never Walter himself, well not properly. He'd seen photos of him in the papers and news footage of him leaving the hospital, but he'd never seen him in the flesh like this, back in his own life, in his own suit and tie, out of the news and back at work.

He had been, he admitted to himself, slightly excited by the prospect. In fact, wasn't it this that had led him into acting so rashly? So easy, wasn't it, to look him up on the net, find out where he worked, ask at Reception if he could see him? They'd sent him out just like that, as if he was just anybody. And so he'd got his first face-to-face look at Walter Kovak.

And yet ... like someone meeting their favourite movie star and finding out that he or she was shorter than expected, or their skin wasn't as perfect as it was up on screen, that they were annoying or tongue-tied or rude, or worse that they were old—that they were, in fact, ordinary, everyday people— Michael was aware of a feeling of acute disappointment. Here was a man who had survived a major accident, a man who had survived against the most alarming, the most stupendous odds, and yet face to face he was a totally ordinary bloke, kind of daggy, working in an insurance firm. There was nothing special about him at all.

3.
THE ODDS OF DYING

Walter was washing up his mug in a small, drab kitchenette when Mick walked in with another young man very much in the Mick mould, a face that Walter hadn't noticed around Equity Insurance before. Mick was younger than Walter, perhaps in his mid to late twenties. He belonged to a group of young men, mostly Aussie, who all went to bars together after work on a Friday night, or out for lunchtime curries, or for a Red Bull and a smoke, or whatever it was they did when they disappeared from the office. He was pasty faced and flabby, and wore loose-fitting, slightly too-big trousers halfway down his arse, a half untucked shirt and loosened tie. He had a general air of not caring about the job (not that Walter would hold that against him particularly) and not being particularly intelligent, but he was, Walter thought with a sigh, the type who would get ahead.

Walter didn't much like Mick. He didn't like these sorts of young men. He didn't understand them. The way they spoke for example.

Hey, mate.

Alright?

All good.

Much on?

Yeah. You?

Enough.

That's the way.

How could they go on like that, with a whole string of non-sequiturs, and then move away from each other as if they'd had some sort of conversation? Walter didn't get it. He just didn't get it.

Mick spoke to him with a smirk on his face and in his voice.

'Walter. This is David. He's new. With me over in wealth management.'

'Hey, mate.' David said.

Here we go, Walter thought.

'Hello,' he said with a polite smile. 'Good to meet you. I hope you settle in OK.'

With that Walter presumed it was all over, so he dropped his eyes and made a movement indicating he wanted to pass out of the kitchenette, but Mick did not move aside. He stood blocking Walter's way out of the pokey little space, subtly menacing through merely being so stolidly in the way with no intention of moving. He was, Walter thought, just like a grown-up schoolyard bully and even though it was a long time since he'd been at school, he instantly remembered the prickle of being singled out.

'So, Walt,' Mick said. 'Got time for a quick one?'

So that's what it was about.

'Well, not really. I've got to finish the ...' He again made as if to step between them, but again Mick didn't stand aside and so he fell back.

'Come on. A quickie. Come onnn, Walt. No good holding out on us.'

Mick eyed David and smirked.

'Oh, OK. OK. A quick one. Why not,' Walter said.

'Right. Dave, pick a method of dying. Anything you like. Anything.'

'A what?'

'A method of dying. Walt's a gun with odds. Knows them all. Don't you Walter?'

'Well, a lot of them, yes. It's really not that unusual.' It wasn't unusual. He worked in life insurance in actuaries—of course it wasn't unusual. Well, maybe a little.

Dying was, of course, a certainty, but Walter knew the precise odds of dying by different methods. The big killers were heart disease which killed one in five of the population, cancer one in seven, and stroke one in twenty nine. But he also knew off by heart the odds of dying in other ways, right down to the more obscure methods of bee sting and lightning strike.

'Come on,' Mick said to David. 'Pick.'

'Ummm. Righto. Arrr—car accident.'

Mick smacked his hands over his eyes.

'Too easy!' he said.

But Walter was warming up into it now.

'Fatal on site, or delayed?' he asked.

'Delayed?' David asked.

'He means died after—in hospital,' Mick answered.

'Err—fatal.'

'Driver or passenger?' Walter smiled now.

'Err—driver.'

'Based on current statistics, the lifetime odds of a driver dying on site after having been in a car accident are one in two hundred and forty four. So, for every two hundred and forty four people now living, one of them will die, whenever they die, in a car accident.'

'In Victoria? Or Australia wide.'

'That's Australia-wide. You're a bit safer in Victoria. Here only one in two hundred and *seventy five* people will die in a car accident.'

Dave was nodding, thinking. After a second he clicked his fingers and pointed at Walter.

'What if you don't drive?' he asked, as if he'd found a loophole.

'Then you're unlikely to be that one person,' Walter said dryly. He shrugged. 'There are plenty of caveats, and being at risk of dying in a certain way isn't the same as the odds of dying in that way. Risk varies with age and location and medical history. And of course the odds skew if there is an unexpected medical epidemic say, or a natural disaster. The odds of dying are based on generic overall number crunching, but they're incredibly accurate all the same.'

'Right,' Dave said.

'Good one, Walt.'

They were impressed, certainly, but there were still smirks across their faces. Walter knew that even though he had an impressive memory and had such detailed statistical information at his fingertips, he was, nonetheless, to them, an oddity. He made another move to leave the kitchenette, but again they remained standing in his way. He couldn't get past them without pushing past, without crossing a line somewhere, breaking some rule of workplace etiquette—the 'I pretend not to know you're taking the piss and you pretend not to be taking the piss' rule.

Don't make me push past, he thought.

They just looked at him.

And suddenly Walter thought of the moment on the train station platform that morning when he had stood rooted to the spot, unable to enter the train, and people had met his eye, looked at him. He blushed at the memory. Sometimes he felt as if the worst thing in the world was to be looked at, sometimes he felt as if it bruised him.

*

Walter usually arrived at work at 8.00am, had his morning tea at 10.30am and his lunch at 12.30pm. That morning, having arrived at 8.45am, he found his routine out of whack—he had his morning cup of tea at 10.45am and he only noticed the time on his computer, grabbed his coat and headed out for lunch at 1.10pm.

Walter regularly bought his lunch at a sandwich shop around the corner from Equity, and he invariably got a ham, cheese, tomato sandwich and an orange juice. If the weather was bad he would eat in at one of the little tables down the back of the shop, or at the bench that lined the shop window. If the weather was good he would take his lunch and go to a nearby churchyard. It wasn't that Walter was in any way religious—he had been brought up to be a good Catholic, as most Poles were, but had abandoned religion as soon as he moved out of home. He visited this little church, hidden away behind a spiked fence between two hi-rise buildings, because it had a small public garden that nobody seemed to know about. He enjoyed coming there to sit and eat his lunch on one of the benches under the straggly plane trees, watching the religious pass into and out of the church while the scrappy little city sparrows hopped around his feet and darted in for crumbs.

The sandwich shop was owned by a middle-aged couple and amazingly, given his track record with shop people, the second time he had gone there, so long ago now, the woman had remembered his order and had asked if he wanted the same thing. Walter was impressed that she had got it right, flattered and amazed that she had remembered him, and he nodded and agreed, even though he probably would have ordered something else. From that day on he had 'the regular' no matter what he actually felt like.

When it came time to pay for his lunch, Walter realised he was missing his wallet. He felt in his hip pocket, then patted the rest of his pants pockets, both front and back—nothing. He checked his coat pockets but again, nothing.

Perhaps he had left it in the office?

He apologised quickly to the woman who had made his sandwich and said they should keep it aside, he would be back shortly, that he'd left his wallet behind. The woman told him he could pay another day, but now that he knew he'd misplaced his wallet he wanted to find it as soon as possible.

It took him only five minutes to get back to his desk at Equity, but there was no sign of his wallet. He checked his briefcase—again no wallet.

Odd.

Perhaps it was in the car? He thought back to arriving that morning, late and a bit flustered. Had he taken his wallet out of his briefcase then? Perhaps to put away the car park ticket he took from the machine on entering?

It was only a quick trot a half block to the multi-level car park. When he got there he entered the lift, pressed a button for his level, then stood back and noticed a sign advising patrons that valuables should not be left visible in cars as this encouraged theft. As the lift ascended slowly to the top of the car park Walter stared at the poster. It had a tacky clipart picture, a silhouette of a hooded man with a crowbar, and a red circle with a line diagonally across the middle over the top of him. As the door dinged open Walter felt a sort of resignation wash over him.

Great, he thought. *Just great.*

He went to his car. The driver's side window had been smashed. Little cubes of shattered glass were scattered all over the driver's side seat and the floor. He peered in through the shattered window but could see no sign of his wallet. It also appeared that his CD player had been stolen. Ibiza Summer with it? Possibly.

He went to the passenger side, opened the door and got in, fastidiously brushing some of the broken glass off the seat first. He checked the glove box but found it empty. No wallet. No CDs. He sat there looking from the broken window to the gaping hole where his CD player had been. He felt this was just his luck. He said to himself, in his head, feeling sorry for himself: *The story of my life.* He sighed, and as he breathed in again he noticed something. He sniffed a couple of times, then wrinkled up his nose.

What was that smell?

He leaned across towards the driver's side seat and sniffed. Again he smelt it, but not noticeably stronger. He looked into the back seat. There was nothing in there. He sniffed again, and again there was the smell but again not noticeably stronger.

What was it? It was definitely unpleasant and somehow human. Was it the smell of the man who had smashed the window of his car and sat, presumably, on the driver's side seat on top of the glass? Yes, he thought, it was the smell of perspiration, unwashed clothes, stale cigarette smoke, and perhaps, he sniffed again, the slightest suggestion, somewhere in there, of human or animal faeces. Dog shit?

Walter got out of the car rather rapidly and returned to work. There, he went directly to the toilets and washed his hands—thoroughly. After a while of scrubbing he dried them under the air drier, wiped them together a little, then gently sniffed them. Sniffed again. They seemed OK but …

He sniffed at the cuff of his suit jacket. *Oh crap.*

*

Back at his desk, in his shirt sleeves, Walter got on the phone and began all the necessary arrangements with a definite sense of ennui. First he called the police and reported the break-in. After being placed on hold for some time, a constable asked a lot of questions in a desultory manner and didn't seem, Walter thought, all that hopeful of any outcome other than a lot of paperwork. Then Walter rang his bank to arrange the cancellation of his credit card and VicRoads to notify them of his stolen driver's licence. Both also put him on hold, but at least his bank notified him of his 'place in the queue' and how long the wait would be. This didn't serve to cheer him up any.

While on hold this last time, Dev put his head up over Walter's carpeted cubicle wall.

'You do work here, don't you?' he asked. 'I mean, for us?'

*

Driving home after work was, to put it mildly, a bit of a challenge for Walter. Usually he enjoyed being alone in the car—it gave him at least the pretence of isolation from everything else, from other people, from other road users. Sure, in peak hour he was hemmed in amongst his fellow man, bumper to bumper, but at the same time he felt completely separate from them all, removed, like a child who puts his hands over his eyes in order to hide, because if he can't see you, well obviously you can't see him. That morning, after the incident at the train station, his car had been a welcome little cocoon for him, a hermetically sealed environment where he could control the climate at the press of a button, contact whomever he wished via mobile phone, listen to whatever music he liked. It was so gloriously private and isolated and, the word came unexpectedly, *safe*.

But now things were different. The window had been smashed, there was a gaping hole instead of a driver's side window, and thus no way he could seal himself in. There was no CD player and no CDs, so there was no music. More, there was that smell—that foreign, dirty, alien smell of someone else, some unwanted intruder now gone, but who had left his stink.

He turned his head towards the open window and took a good long sniff of the outside air.

*

Maggie didn't have a job as such. Well, she did, but it wasn't the same sort of eight to five grind in the city that Walter endured. She worked in a fashion boutique on a small shopping strip in Fitzroy North, a suburb a good hour away from Wintergardens by car, an inner city suburb more wealthy and artsy. Her hours weren't as prescribed as Walter's and her income was erratic. Walter was never sure, to be honest, how often she worked or how much she made. It wasn't, he thought to himself (very definitely only to himself) a real job, as the boutique was owned by a friend of hers from school, and he suspected the arrangement was more an excuse for them to spend time together and go on the occasional trip overseas. They called them 'buying trips'.

Maggie's closet was packed tight with clothes, although she usually seemed to Walter to be wearing the exact same thing. She looked stylish and very finished, but also sort of simple and severe. Black and grey featured prominently in her wardrobe, although that was not unusual for Melbourne women. She also wore small patterned scarves tied tight around her throat, a look that Walter had always admired—it seemed to him vaguely 60s and even a little bit airline-hostess. He hadn't shared this with Maggie—he wasn't sure she would appreciate it.

When Walter got home that night, Maggie was there, which wasn't always the case, and was cooking dinner, something else that wasn't always the case. Often she stayed late at work, or was out a little late doing errands or perhaps visiting with friends, or with Arlette, but the arrangement was that whoever arrived home first began dinner. It was usually him—he was a competent if unimaginative cook. It was a simple, common-sense, domestic understanding, but sometimes it felt to Walter as if their home life was slightly disjointed, as if their lives overlapped like a Venn diagram, rather than were lived together.

He told her immediately about the car being broken into, confessed it almost like a penitent school-boy. He was remembering her phone call of that morning—she had needed the car as her little runabout was in having body-work done. She had ticked him off about it. He expected her to say something about that, perhaps say that if he hadn't taken the car it wouldn't have happened. It would be the sort of thing she might bring up, but she didn't. She was annoyed about the car being broken into, certainly, but nothing more. She was not dismayed as Walter had been. Her annoyance seemed to be about the inconvenience of fixing the car, the time it would be off the road, the bother of claiming insurance, not because she felt it in any way an affront or a worry. She seemed to be of the opinion it was just the sort of thing that happened, annoying of course, but a fact of life. Little bingles and scratches and fender-benders—they happened. She herself was the kind of driver to park by touch.

It was only later, during dinner, that Walter mentioned the smell.

Maggie stopped chewing and looked at him, really looked at him for the first time since he'd walked through the door. It made him realise how little she actually did look at him these days—only when he'd done something surprising, and perhaps he didn't surprise her much any more.

'A smell?' she asked. 'What smell?'

'There's a smell.'

'Is there? What's it smell like?'

'I don't know,' Walter said. 'I don't ... know. It just smells dirty ... unclean. I don't know ...'

Maggie wrinkled her nose.

'I thought I could smell something.'

Walter's face froze. After a second he put his fork down, swallowed and tensed his neck muscles in his collar. His nostrils twitched. Was it still there? The smell? Was it? He couldn't smell anything—but what if he had got used to it and no longer smelt it on himself?

'Excuse me,' he said, then got up from the table and left the room.

*

A couple of minutes later Walter was in the shower, the warm water streaming over him. He scrubbed his body with a face-washer that was foaming with too much soap.

In the middle of his shower the water went suddenly cold and he stepped gingerly out from under it, bashing his shoulder and forehead on the glass of the shower-screen.

Maggie must have turned on the hot water to do the dishes or something. Surely she knew that it affected the temperature of the water in the shower when she did that? Walter suspected that she knew alright, that she must know, and that she did it anyway, in fact on purpose, specifically when he was in the shower.

He adjusted the hot water, waited, tested the temperature, then stepped cautiously back under.

'Bitch,' he said under his breath.

*

A little later Walter came into the kitchen, freshly scrubbed, redolent of the smell of soap and shampoo, in his pyjamas, dressing gown and slippers—it was too early for pyjamas perhaps, but he wasn't going to get dressed again now. He was, rather incongruously, also wearing rubber gloves.

Maggie was standing at the sink slowly drying the dishes. More accurately she was taking a break from drying the dishes, standing with the tea-towel over her shoulder, smoking, staring over the bench into the room beyond, watching television—some reality show she wasn't really interested in.

Walter went to the cupboard under the sink, pulled out the bin and took the lid off. Then he picked up a partly full ashtray and held it towards Maggie, making a distasteful little face. Maggie looked at him for a second then butted her cigarette out in the ashtray with two big stabs, leaving it smouldering.

Walter made sure the butt was properly out then emptied the ashtray into the garbage bin, tied off the rubbish bag and lifted it out of the bin. Passing through the laundry, he picked up the clothes that he had worn that day—the jacket, trousers and the shirt, the underwear even—and took them with the kitchen rubbish to the wheelie bin at the side of the house. He threw the whole lot in there and took the bin to the nature strip. Then, after a moment, he took each of the rubber gloves off with a snap and threw them both in the bin as well.

'There,' he said to himself. 'Done.'

He could almost have dusted his hands symbolically, but he decided against it—he wasn't one for extravagant gestures.

4.
KNIFE ATTACK ON CROWDED TRAIN

By the time Walter went to bed his mood had lifted slightly. His car had been broken into, sure, but it was now safely in the garage. His credit cards and licence had been stolen, but he had put a halt on them all and was getting new ones. Soon the car window would be fixed, the interior of the car cleaned. Tomorrow morning the garbage would be collected and the clothes he had worn that day would be gone, and with them any possible remnants, any last whiff of that smell would be gone also.

He lay there straight and still in bed, the sheet folded neatly over the top of the doona, his arms outside the covers, his hands folded together on his stomach.

Maggie was in the ensuite bathroom. She was humming a tune and obviously in good humour for some reason. Walter wasn't really able to follow her moods much any more, but if she was humming it was a good sign and he was content with that. It added to his general lift in mood.

All he had to do now, Walter thought, was put that man and his ridiculous warning out of his mind. *Don't get on the next train.* Walter lay there, thinking about it. Pondering. It wasn't the warning that bothered him so much, it was his reaction. He had really behaved most incalculably, being so rattled by that silly warning. Safe in bed, calm and tightly tucked in, he thought back to his stick-insect-like indecision that morning on the platform, but he thought about it ruefully and without any heat in his cheeks. It was more, Walter knew, than just what the man had said, as unexpected as that was, it was the location in which he had said it—a train platform, with a train pulling up in front of them, the noise and the wind along the platform, the sensations. He had to hold himself in, as it were, especially tight when the train came in along the platform like that, even on a normal day, but he had been doing so well for so long now. He thought he was over all that, over, at any rate, the more overt symptoms. So perhaps his response, his behaviour, his reaction was not so incalculable, given the circumstances. Still slightly disappointing though.

Then his thoughts meandered off in another direction.

Funny. If it wasn't for that man and his warning, he would never have driven to work, and none of the stuff with the car would have happened …

But before he could think more along these or any other lines, Maggie came out of the bathroom. Her face was glistening and moist with cream. She wore an old, thin, too-big t-shirt and actually, Walter thought, looked quite sexy in a daggy, not-trying type way, with her hair up in a messy bun and her face all dewy and glistening.

*

Maggie turned off the ensuite light with her elbow and took a step towards the bed, then suddenly stopped dead and made a half-laugh sound in her nose. *Walter*, she thought—*look at him!* Up and down, straight as a rod, tucked in neat and tidy and snug as a bug in a rug. What a sight. Suddenly, with a pang of surprise, she remembered how she had once found his sheer asexuality sexually attractive. It was a perversion of response she hadn't experienced for some time and it delighted her, in and of itself, but also because she was glad she still had the capacity to feel it.

'Comfortable?' she asked in a light, teasing tone.

Walter looked nonplussed.

'Yes,' he said. 'Why?'

'No reason,' she smiled and continued over towards the bed.

*

Not very much later that night Walter and Maggie were having sex. It wasn't very exciting sex, perhaps, being as it was missionary position and strictly by the book, but it was sex all the same. It had been Maggie who had initiated it. Usually it was these days. She had been the one to initiate it their first time together, and that's how it had been for most of their sexual life, apart from that brief honeymoon period when they were first married and Walter, well, lost his head really, with the whole idea of sex-on-tap. But after a while it had seemed only natural to Walter that he take his sexual-Greenwich-Time from her. When the opportunity arose, he was not one to say no.

Unfortunately Walter was unable to stop thinking about, of all things, Mick and the new guy at the office, and the silly conversation they had earlier that day in the kitchenette, the conversation about the odds of dying. They had asked, after the car accident odds, for another go. Mick had asked this, saying that 'car accident' was too simple, too easy. He wanted something more unusual, he said, something that would be harder, more of a challenge for Walter, something like *autoerotic asphyxiation.*

Walter was instantly sure that this was what they'd had in mind all along, that they had possibly even discussed asking this exact thing before they came to the kitchenette. Aware as he was that it was exactly the reaction they were hoping for, he was unable to stop himself from giving it—he blushed furiously.

'We don't ... we don't have st-stat-statistics for that kind of ...' Not only had he blushed, he also stuttered and stammered and left his sentence unfinished. His reaction was extreme and beyond his control, and obviously highly amusing to Mick and the new guy.

'What's that?' the new guy asked Mick innocently—not very convincingly.

'You know,' Mick answered. 'Choking yourself to make your orgasm more, you know,' he made a fist, 'intense.'

'You're kidding me. Does it work?'

'Oh yeah mate. Yeah. Bit of pressure on the carotid—is it the carotid, Walter? And you're off like a cracker, mate. Every time. Guarantee it!'

'Come on fellas,' Walter tried. 'Come on … that's enough …'

In bed, having sex with his wife, Walter squinted his eyes, concentrated on his thrusts and tried to think about something else, someone else, not Mick, not the new guy and not autoerotic strangulation, but he couldn't help it. He kept seeing flashes of naked men with a stocking tied around their scrotum, hanging by the neck from closet doorknobs in anonymous hotel rooms. It was at this point that underneath him Maggie began to moan more convincingly. Apparently she was starting to enjoy herself—finally.

He couldn't help himself, couldn't help flashing back to one final thing from earlier in the day. He was back at his desk, his blush had subsided after the kitchenette episode and his breathing was returning to normal, but after a second or two he heard them, heard Mick and the new guy in the kitchenette. Whispering? No, not whispering. What was it? He cocked his ear and listened harder. Then he realised what it was—a soft, furtive, sound coming from the kitchenette—they were laughing at him.

With a grunt of extra effort he successfully blacked the whole kitchenette experience from his mind and coincidentally brought his wife to orgasm.

*

That night Walter had the dream again. He woke with a small cry and sat bolt upright in bed, a sheen of sweat over him. Maggie was awake beside him and manoeuvring herself up on one elbow. She said nothing, just watched him, too bleary eyed and tired to display any particular expression.

'OK OK,' Walter said. He got out of bed and padded across the carpet. Maggie re-settled herself under the covers.

Walter went to his study and clicked on the light. It was a single uncovered bulb in the centre of the ceiling, and it illuminated a room that was very Walter. There was a bookshelf against one wall with mostly non-fiction books, history books, biographies of political or wartime leaders, a set of encyclopaedias, other random reference books and a large number of back-issues of National Geographic. It was an incredibly tidy bookcase. Along the other wall was a desk with an upright PC, monitor, keyboard, mouse and printer. There were also, just like his desk at work, various stationery items laid out as if rigidly spaced—pens in a plastic holder, magic-tape, stapler. Otherwise there was nothing—no pictures on the wall, no pin-board of postcards, no standard lamp for a more subdued lighting option, no wastepaper basket, no mess to put in one, no coffee cups, no slippers kicked off under the desk. It was so sparsely furnished, so tidy, and in the glare of the bare bulb so flat, that it looked like a *trompe l'oeil* painting of a room rather than a real room. In spite of this, or perhaps because of it, Walter found his study comforting.

He sat down at his desk heavily, as usual straight-backed and flat-footed, ran his hands through his hair, damp with sweat, then rubbed at his eyes and temples with the heel of each hand. He took a deep breath and blew it out noisily, through his lips, like a horse. He felt ... how did he feel? His heart was beating quicker for a start. He could feel it, feel the pump of blood in his neck and the inside of his elbows. He let it go for a while, just sat there and felt the *foom-foom* of his blood, sat with it until it quietened down. When that had happened he got up and went across to the bookcase. He drew his forefinger across a number of the spines, none of them cracked or broken, of course, all aligned perfectly with the edge of the shelves, until he found what he was looking for—a small book, smaller than most of the rest, slimmer. He took the book out and held it for a moment. It was the size of a small paperback, covering almost exactly his palm and extended fingers, where he let it sit for a moment, as if he took comfort in the weight and size of it. He then flicked through the book with one thumb, fanning the pages carefully. He could smell the paper, the slightly chemical smell of bleached stock, an unusual smell, stronger than the smell of his other books. The pages, blurred as he fanned them, were not printed thickly with paragraphs of text but instead contained tables, lists and numbers in a regular, generic font, widely spaced. It did not look or smell like something that was commercially printed and distributed for sale. It wasn't. It was published by a group that called itself the National Australian Committee for Safety and it contained statistics for each and every recorded death in Australia between Federation and the current year. The title on the front of the book was *The Odds of Dying*. In short, it predicted how Australian people would die.

Walter didn't have to look it up. He already knew that the odds of dying in a train crash were one in sixty five thousand eight hundred and seventy. He couldn't work out whether that number seemed like a little or a lot.

*

The next morning Walter was back on the Wintergardens train platform waiting for the 7.15am express. It was Thursday so he was wearing his Thursday suit—navy, three button jacket, double vent, single pleated pants, 40% off, but almost six years ago now. He would have to go to a menswear store at some point and replace Wednesday's suit—charcoal, three button jacket, single vent, flat front pant—the one he'd thrown in the bin the previous day. He carried his briefcase and also had the daily newspaper, rolled in plastic, under his arm. There was no sun-shower that morning.

The temperature was mild enough and the sky blue, so he did not carry an umbrella.

Again there was the motley assortment of his Wintergardens fellow commuters around him. Some of them carried papers and briefcases, or laptops, the occasional one a backpack, or a packed lunch in a plastic bag, leftovers perhaps in a Tupperware container. Some smoked, but not under the covered areas of the platform where it was not allowed. Some talked on mobile phones or listened to their ipods.

Walter looked up and down the platform, looking for the man who had spoken to him the previous day, but there was no sign of him. Not that he could remember what the man looked like, not really. He was older, Walter remembered that, maybe edging towards sixty, with grey hair, an ordinary sort of face, clean-shaven. Walter found he couldn't remember details. He felt sure he'd recognise him if he saw him again, but he wasn't sure he could accurately describe him, which was unexpected and a little unnerving.

Even though he'd only done it one minute ago, he looked at the platform clock. It was 7.14am. Then he looked down the tracks. No train. He double-checked the time on his wristwatch. It was correct and the train was late again.

Walter juggled the newspaper out from underneath his arm, took it out of the plastic wrapping, which he discarded in a nearby bin, then set his briefcase between his feet, shook the newspaper open, bent the kinks out of it and looked at the front page. The headline gave him a nasty jolt. KNIFE ATTACK ON CROWDED TRAIN.

Walter scanned the story quickly. Apparently the previous morning a young man with a knife had lashed out at commuters on a packed peak-hour train. The attack had been random and unprovoked, although many commuters interviewed afterwards said the young man had appeared to be nervous. One witness had said he looked 'off his nut'. The young man had been subdued by a number of commuters who exited the train with him at North Melbourne and handed him over to station security who held him until the police arrived. The story seemed to end, but there was more, Walter saw, on page three. He turned to page three.

'Which train?' he asked the newspaper.

He read on. Six people sustained injuries and one man was taken to hospital where he later died. The names of the victims and suspect were not reported.

Then he saw it. The knife attack had happened yesterday on the 7.15am express train from Wintergardens to the City—his train.

Don't get on the next train, the man had said, and if it weren't for that warning Walter would have been on that train, his regular train, and he could even have been in the carriage, the one with the man with the knife. Possibly. Why not? Pressed in, packed in like a sardine right near this young man who attacked unprovoked, lashed out with a knife. He could perhaps have been one of the people injured. He could have been that man, the one whose name they hadn't released, the man taken to hospital where he later died.

Walter gave a start and crumpled the newspaper between his hands. The train had pulled into the station and the sudden noise of it, the wind around his knees, had surprised him out of all proportion. He smoothed the newspaper, folded it, put it under his arm and picked up his briefcase. The warning beeps sounded, the train doors were opened by passengers from inside, a couple of people stepped off, then those waiting began filing on. In a few seconds it was his turn and he stepped onto the carriage in a determined, stolid way, as if holding himself very tight and focussed. He found a seat and sat there rigid and well-arranged, his briefcase square on his lap, his newspaper neatly folded and square on top of that. His face was fixed.

Taken to hospital, he was thinking, *where he later died.* The phrase chilled him. The death bit, certainly, but even the first part—*taken to hospital.* He didn't like hospitals. He didn't want to have anything to do with hospitals. Not after last time. Not much had been wrong with him then, not really, not physically; nothing that wouldn't mend at home, but they'd kept him there, for observation they said. He'd hated it. It had been more than just the smell of the place, the smell of sickness partially disguised by disinfectant and a sort of chemical smell which he thought of as the scent of medicine, it was also the attention he received from the staff, many of whom came to look at him, just look at him—OK, examine him, they said—as if he was something odd and unexpected and out of the way. He didn't need examining. There was nothing wrong with him, nothing special about him, nothing to observe. There had been others too, outsiders, reporters, one time a man with a camera, although he was escorted off very quickly. *Paparazzi*, Walter thought, and he thought it as he would have said it, with an intonation of irony, of ridicule, of distaste, and of pure disbelief that he, Walter Kovak, should be hounded by paparazzi.

Behind these thoughts on hospitals and paparazzi, like an incongruous soundtrack, Walter could hear the sound of the train, *rickety-clack, rickety-clack.* Nobody else in the carriage heard the sound. Of course they did, but they didn't notice it as Walter did. He heard it all the time, listened for it, heard it in his head perhaps louder than it really was. *Rickety-clack, rickety-clack,* like the *foom-foom* of his pulse.

5. MICHAEL EVERAARDT'S LUCKY BREAK

A year ago Michael Everaardt had been a young journalist not long out of university with a job at a free daily newspaper. After being shunted around various positions that included very little meaningful writing, he unexpectedly found himself being promoted to sub-editor, although what this actually meant was that he proofread the work of others and cut it to length to fit the space allocated. The only writing he did himself in his role as sub was to make up headlines. He and three other disgruntled colleagues of around the same age took great pride in coming up with punning headlines over long afternoons at the pub downstairs from their office. Some of their headlines were alliterative, some were a play on words or names, some contained groaningly obvious sexual innuendo, some were better than the articles following them. In the end, he became fed up with wasting his time and what he considered—he was Gen Y after all—his talent. He went home one day all amped up and ready to resign, full of new ideas about what he could do. His girlfriend at the time, a pretty girl called Rosie, a law grad doing her articles, had tried to convince him to put his energies into something outside his regular day-to-day work.

'Like what?' he'd asked stupidly.

'Actually write something, maybe?'

It had been a good idea, of course. Simple, like all brilliant ideas were. Bless Rosie. He really should have done something about keeping her. She was a keeper, more sweet than sexy, bit mumsy maybe, but the thought of a long-term, serious relationship was, at the time, a little far away from where he was at. Of course he wanted to meet great girls, keepers, but he didn't really want to keep them when he had them. He felt there was some unfinished business work-wise to get going before anything would be possible on the personal front. So he'd taken Rosie's advice and cut back on the after-work drinks with his mates at the pub, which more often than not had continued through the afternoon. (He started at 6.00am, but finished at 2.00pm—a dangerous time to be let loose with nothing much to do and a whole lot of mates to do it with.) Instead he pulled his finger out and actually researched and wrote a number of articles which he submitted to some of the bigger newspapers. He was aiming for the magazine-style articles regularly featured in weekend supplements. He assumed this was a difficult area to break into, but weren't they all? He felt he had to persevere at something, anything that wasn't copy editing and writing smart-arse headlines. But none of the articles were picked up.

He got his big break totally by accident, by being in the right place at the right time—exactly the sort of thing he used to hate hearing about from others, but didn't mind so much when it happened to him. He had been only half a block away when an overpass collapsed onto an outbound Wintergardens line train. It took officials some time and a thorough investigation afterwards to be absolutely certain what had actually happened. It appeared that a truck which was too high had attempted to travel on the road that ran alongside the rail line underneath the overpass, had hit the height barrier, swerved and overturned, shunting into one of the supports of the overpass, which had in turn caused the overpass, a major one, with two lanes and a turning lane each way, to collapse on the train, crushing one carriage entirely and de-railing those behind. A number of cars and their drivers also came down in the collapse, and although there were a large number of casualties, the worst hit was the carriage directly underneath the collapsed overpass, which was crushed like a tin can.

Michael of course, had known nothing of any of this at the time. He had merely been visiting with a mate of his and was walking the half block back towards his car when he heard a rumble and felt the ground shake briefly, before seeing at the end of the street, which abutted the train line, a billow of dust spreading slowly in the air.

After a second he automatically started a shambling run towards the end of the street and fumbled out his mobile phone to call emergency services. As he rounded the corner it wasn't, at first, immediately obvious what had happened. It was a still day, no breeze at all—all he could see was a billow of thick dust and through it a mess of rubble. After a moment the dust began to clear and he could see cars were amongst the rubble, half-squashed or buried, one jutting out at an odd angle, as if rearing up. He couldn't see anything of the train carriage underneath the rubble but knew it must be there because of the rest of the train which was concertinaed up in a long derailed zigzag leading away from the rubble and dust.

In the moments it took to become aware of what he was seeing, he also began to hear people calling out, mostly from the derailed train carriages. He saw them, then, through the dust, scrambling from the carriages further down the track.

Something automatic took over inside him. He went to assist and found himself helping all afternoon, wherever he could be of use. There were so many people, people who had been in the accident, and others, bystanders, people who had heard and had come to see and help. He lost track of time and of anything his own body was feeling, hunger or fatigue. His emotions, he also found, had been dulled. He saw some things he'd never seen before, like a dead body, not just one, more than one, and yet didn't feel a thing.

At one point he helped an older woman away from the wreckage. She was dressed in what would once have been a neat skirt, shirt and cardigan, but was now torn and dirtied. She had somehow managed to hold onto her handbag through the impact and confusion afterwards, and she carried it hooked over her forearm. When Michael first saw her she was picking her way along the tracks. Something was wrong with her head, though—she had a lot of blood on one side of her face and she kept leaning to one side, stumbling, as if her balance was severely affected. He went to her and took her by the arm, held her tight, steadied her steps and assisted her down the tracks away from the site of the accident, where he delivered her to the attention and care of others. She looked him direct in the eye, then smiled and nodded in a tight, reserved way. 'Thank you,' she said graciously, then keeled over dead.

He found out later that she had received a severe blow to the head and body on impact and died of extensive internal haemorrhage, was probably dying as she picked her way across the stones, was virtually dead from the moment it happened.

There were more people and other deaths, too many for him to process then and there, but perhaps the most horrible thing about that day, not that he felt this until a long while afterwards, was that it was for him a godsend, all thanks to a couple of seconds that he wasn't in the least proud of. In those moments immediately following the accident, the moments of stunned shock before he could get close enough to help, before anyone knew exactly what had happened, when there was just a huge billowing cloud of dust hovering in the air around the accident site, Michael did what so many people in possession of a mobile phone might do—he snapped off a couple of photos. As such he was, it turned out, one of the only people to capture the immediate aftermath of the accident on camera. When he got home that day he remembered, with a first twinge of that guilt, the photos he had taken. He called them up on his phone and looked through them. There were only three. Two were simply of the cloud of dust and the rubble just discernable through it, but the third of them was slightly different. In this shot was a man, seen in silhouette only, seen imperfectly through the cloud of dust, a man who appeared to be getting to his feet right in the middle of the rubble, his legs slightly bent, his shoulders hunched and his head down. He seemed, amazingly, to be climbing directly out of the very spot where the accident had happened, the epicentre.

Michael knew from talk on the accident site that there had been only one survivor from the carriage directly under the collapse of the overpass, and that, miraculously, this man had climbed free without assistance almost immediately after the collapse. It was a one in a million chance, they were saying, for someone to survive such a collapse, and yet it had happened. One man only out of what had proven later to be a total of sixteen passengers in that carriage, one man only had survived. Dazed, scratched and bloody, but largely unscathed. He had been taken immediately to hospital. His name, they said, was Walter Kovak, and Michael, although he hadn't realised it at the time, had a picture on his phone of this Walter Kovak climbing so miraculously out of the wreckage.

He took his phone to the computer, booted up and set about downloading the photos. He felt buzzy with excitement, felt also, idiotically, that his phone was going to crash, delete everything, explode or something, before he could download the photo, and that the picture of the single survivor from the crushed carriage would be lost. He was clumsy and impatient, all thumbs, but he downloaded the photo without incident and immediately backed it up onto a USB stick, then emailed it to both his work and personal email accounts so that it sat in four different locations.

The photo safe, he took a breath, got himself a drink, a beer, cracked his knuckles in an exaggerated way, for fun and for the chutzpah needed for his next step, and sat down to compose an email to the editor of the major tabloid daily newspaper of the state, offering them his own eye-witness account of the accident, interviews with a number of survivors, and to top it all off, a photo, the only photo in all probability, of the single survivor from the crushed carriage. He attached the photo and sent the email.

He had an answer within a half hour. He had a deadline for his eye-witness account, a promise they would consider submissions from him in the days to follow, and an arrangement to use his photograph on the front page of the next morning edition of the newspaper.

Michael laughed when he read it. He felt incredible. In his imagination, someone, somewhere, having received his email, having seen that photo, had yelled: 'Stop the press!' Oh, he hoped they had.

He finished his beer, decided not to have another until he was over the hump of his eye-witness account, cracked his knuckles again and got down to it.

Much later that night, when he had finished and submitted his piece and had consumed another couple of beers, Michael went out onto his balcony for a smoke. He remembered her out of the blue with a shock of emotion—the woman who had thanked him and then keeled over dead. He slapped his hand to his mouth and was surprised that tears were, almost immediately, in his eyes. For some reason out of everything he had seen that day, everything that had happened to him, it was this woman who had come back to him when he switched his mind off and sat down. He remembered her with astonishing accuracy, her tight little nod, her conventional, polite tone of voice, as if he'd done nothing but help her across the road. He was instantly consumed by a confused flood of emotions—a terrible sadness for this woman, guilt for taking advantage of the situation, and a sort of steely wilfulness, as if he was determined to make the most of it. It was a confusing wash of emotions and he couldn't for a moment pick them apart or cope with them. So he sat there on his balcony in the darkness with the fingertips of his left hand pressed to his lips, his cigarette in his right, and simply allowed himself to cry.

He was young enough, resilient enough, perhaps simple enough, for those tears to be quite enough of a release. He slept brilliantly afterwards and the next day he woke as if he'd just had a couple of energy drinks, instantly awake and punchy, and knowing that something big was out there waiting for him that day. He got out of bed, pulled on his tracksuit pants and a t-shirt and ventured out to the shops.

There it was, outside the newsagent, on the cover, all over the city, his front page, his words, his name, his photo, printed in colour, the browns and beige of the dust cloud, the jagged suggestion of the rubble and the black silhouette of the man getting to his feet. The headline was simply: SOLE SURVIVOR—ironically the headline was the only thing about the front page story that Michael had nothing to do with. Also it was, of course, factually incorrect, the sub in him thought, unless you considered a cordon drawn around the actual carriage that was crushed, and the other people involved not part of the same accident. Even so, he thought, the headline summed up something about the accident that struck a chord with the public. Indeed in the days that followed it turned out that a great amount of attention was focussed on this man, Walter Kovak, the man who had survived against such incredible odds, the sole survivor.

That morning Michael had been very soon inundated with calls from his family, his friends, all sorts of people who had seen his name on the front page and wanted to know if it was him, or if it was another Michael Everaardt. He spent the rest of the day in a haze, alternating between feeling proud, looking again and again at 'his' front page, abstractly nervous about he didn't know what, and sort of antsy and unable to settle to anything.

After some time he realised he hadn't slept more than a couple of hours, or eaten, and thought perhaps he should do a few of these necessary things. He should probably also call work, he thought, and tell them he was sick. There was no way he was going to go to his boring job to sit there sucking back pints and coming up with bullshit headlines today—here was a golden ball of opportunity and he was going to grasp it like fuck.

There were many stories that came out after the accident, some horror stories, certainly, stories of death and loss, but just as many stories of strength and determination, survival, luck. The public wanted to know about those involved, exactly what happened to them, what they felt and what they had been doing just prior to the accident, the moments before impact. Even so, no-one, not a single journalist cracked it for an interview with Walter Kovak. Initially of course he had been in hospital, and interviews were not allowed. There had been grainy photos taken of him in his hospital bed, before the photographer had been found and ejected from the ward, but no interview. There had also been photos taken of his wife entering and leaving the hospital looking like a reluctant celebrity—she had slipped through the waiting photographers every day, in and out, but never, ever stopped or made any comment.

Michael found himself relieved more than anything else that Walter Kovak had successfully avoided being interviewed, because as long as he wasn't interviewed there was the possibility, even if it was only a slim one, that he, Michael Everaardt, could be the one to get that interview—but weeks turned into months, turned into a year, and still it hadn't happened. Perhaps, thought Michael, Walter was a rare bird these days, someone who did not desire publicity in the least.

A year after the accident Michael still had his job as a sub, but was also an occasionally contributing journalist with the daily tabloid. He had also researched, written and sold a couple of articles for the newspaper magazine market. His photograph, used on the cover of the newspaper that day, had been circulated freely online. Michael received only nominal payment for the use of his photo, and it was now in the public domain where, by and large, he was happiest for it to be. The picture had done its duty, had opened up the door for him and he felt thankful, felt that it belonged to him no more than that. He had been commissioned to do follow-up interviews with some of those people he had profiled immediately following the accident. It wasn't made explicit, but it was implied, certainly, that included in the series of interviews would be the sole survivor from the carriage that had been crushed, the man who had not yet given his account of the accident.

6.
BBQ IN WINTERGARDENS

That weekend Walter and Maggie had been asked to a neighbour's barbeque. Walter didn't know Helen and Graeme very well, in fact he didn't know any of his neighbours very well, but Maggie liked Helen, knew some of the others who would be there, and insisted they go. She could have gone by herself, but the people there were mostly couples and she wanted Walter to come, so that was pretty much that.

Walter felt grumpy about having to go. He never liked crowds, never felt at all comfortable in social situations, after-work-drinks or these sorts of neighbourhood barbeques. He was, he knew, an awkward conversationalist. He would plod on through so-called conversations, every comment he made feeling like he was dragging his boots out of a particularly squelchy and sucky patch of mud. It was even worse if there was a pause in the conversation as he would feel compelled to blurt something out just to cover up the awkwardness. He wasn't stupid, he read the newspapers, he knew the sorts of things people talked about, but the way he did it, just plopped it out there, made everyone start and stare at him as if he'd just hocked up a big green golly and spat it on someone's chest or something. You just couldn't win in these sorts of situations—well he couldn't, so he tended to avoid them if at all possible.

Flip it, he didn't want to go to that barbeque and make stupid, useless, squelchy-mud small-talk with a whole lot of people he had nothing in common with other than that they happened to live near each other.

'They're actually quite nice people,' Maggie said to him. She was in the kitchen transferring some bottles of white wine from the fridge to an insulated beverage carry-bag.

Walter looked sharply at her. He hadn't actually said anything but his expression must have been eloquent enough.

'There are millions of quite nice people in the world,' he said airily. 'Doesn't mean I have to be friends with them all.'

'But you aren't friends with any of them.'

Walter was about to disagree with this, but then he stopped. She was right and in his pedantic, fair-minded way he had to acknowledge that, so he merely nodded. He didn't have any what you might call proper friends. He spoke to people, he met people, he did things with people, it seemed like he was almost constantly doing things with other people, but it was always through work, or it was with the neighbours, or Maggie's friends, or Arlette, the voodoo doll, never with anyone of his own choosing.

It wasn't that he minded this in any way, and it wasn't that he saw it as something lacking in himself, not at all. All this superficial interaction, it was just another one of those things that life threw up for him to cope with—social expectations, things that he didn't really want to do and yet had to do, conversations he had to endure, with a slightly tilted head, an expression of interest and a small smile on his face. Sometimes he found that he had blacked out for a minute or two and come back in the middle of a conversation he wasn't listening to, but found himself blandly encouraging.

So what did he want to do? He didn't know. He knew what he didn't want to do, though—he didn't want to go to that barbeque. Even so he walked obediently side-by-side with Maggie, out the door and along the footpath towards Helen's place. She lived a block and a half away.

'Do you have to look so miserable?' Maggie asked on the way.

'Yes,' Walter said.

They walked on—Maggie frowning, Walter sullen.

Across the road Mrs Gunderson was in her yard watering her garden. She used watering her garden as an excuse to keep an eye on the comings and goings up and down the street. As such, water restrictions were the bane of her life and she mostly ignored them. She was a thin, old woman with two Shih Tzu lapdogs, a couple of shaggy little things that were always underfoot. She happily confessed to anyone who would listen that she regularly trod on them—once, she confessed, she had accidentally closed the sliding door on the head of one of them and its eyes had literally popped out. Having closely observed them leave their house and walk along the footpath, Mrs Gunderson finally condescended to wave at them.

Walter and Maggie smiled falsely and waved back.

'Nosy bitch,' Maggie said at the same time as Walter murmured: 'Old busybody.'

They were momentarily united in their fake-smile animosity, and they shared a quick, furtive look. They were so rarely in agreement about anything these days that it surprised them both.

*

Unlike Walter, Maggie switched on in social situations—she came alive and felt energised by them. When Helen opened the front door to them, Maggie plunged through and embraced her warmly with both arms, which she was free to do as she had given Walter the wine and salad to carry. No wonder, he thought sulkily, she had wanted him to come.

Walter trailed behind Maggie into the house and followed the women down a passageway—already they were chattering happily—through a big, warm, messy, friendly kitchen, and from there through double-glass sliding doors thrown open to a large backyard. There was a deck with umbrellas and tables, plus a built-in BBQ which was smoking and sizzling and smelling of meat. There was an expanse of lawn leading down to a fenced-in pool, which it wasn't quite hot enough to be using. The perimeter fence was planted with still immature birch trees which in the slight breeze showed the pale backs of their leaves and made a gentle static sound. All plants in Wintergardens were immature, except of course for the palm trees that had been purchased fully matured for the landscaping around the man-made lake, one of which had died and been replaced a number of times. The Wintergardens palm trees were, oddly, a favourite topic of conversation among residents there. Walter fully expected they would talk about the palm trees at some time that afternoon, about how odd it was that the same one always died, and how much money it must cost to keep replacing it, and how silly it was to do so when that same money should be used on much more useful improvements, like a pedestrian crossing near the shops on the main thoroughfare where so-and-so had almost been clipped by a car just the other day. Walter could hear the conversation in his head and was bored by it before it even began.

Everyone else was on the terrace when Walter and Maggie arrived. There were four or five other couples. The wives, as Walter thought of them, looked the same to him whenever they were caught up together like this in a gaggle. Some of the women there were older, some younger, one of them Asian, but to Walter they were identical, or if not identical then identikit—casual but elegant, with nails and hair and makeup done just so, not too much, but as if they all went to the same hairdresser, bought the same makeup and had the same nail-care routine. They were comfortable with each other, chatty and friendly and somehow 'on'. One of the women caught Walter's eye. Melissa Siska, known simply as Missy, or as Walter thought of her: *the young widow*, uncomfortable with the phrase and all it implied—to him anyway.

Great, he thought with a sinking heart. *She's here.*

Missy's husband, Aristo Siska, had left her with very little other than an unusual surname and two little girls with decidedly Greek colouring—a daily reminder, if one was needed, of his death. Missy worked as a gym instructor and personal trainer and had a slim waist, muscular thighs and calves, and large breasts, the nipples of which, Walter knew from previous sightings, were plainly visible through the Bonds spaghetti strap singlets she wore. He remembered other barbeques, other social occasions with neighbours where he had spent the entire time manoeuvring himself away from Missy, so that their paths would not cross, so that he would not have to speak with her.

Missy's little girls, wearing pink tutus and with gaudy plastic-jewelled clips in their hair ran around the garden with a couple of little boys wearing football jerseys and shorts, whose father presumably barracked for Geelong. Eddie's boys? Walter couldn't quite remember, but he thought Eddie had twin boys. They ran around vaguely down the back of the garden and were told off without ardour every five or six minutes or so.

The husbands also seemed much the same as each other. They were, roughly speaking, all of the same class, although in the supposed classless society of Australia it was, he guessed, more accurate to say they were in the same income bracket. The younger men there may not have been earning as much as the older men, but it was highly probable they would be when they reached their more advanced years. The older men had slightly paunchy bellies and wore polo shirts and long shorts, the younger men, generally fitter and flatter of stomach, wore Havaiana thongs and t-shirts. They all seemed defined by their role of husband and father as much as anything else. They looked mild-tempered, Walter thought, and slightly tame, except perhaps for Eddie who had tattoos and an air of being a bit tough.

Walter caught sight of himself reflected in the glass of the sliding door. He looked exactly the same as the rest of them, wearing as he was his own weekend polo shirt, his chinos and his casual shoes, purchased for him by Maggie for just such occasions, but he was not comforted by this in any way.

The city-bound platform of the Wintergardens train station at 7.15am in the morning was probably more representative of the suburb as a whole, but white bread floats.

It occurred to Walter again.

Why do I feel so different to these people?

*

This was not a new thought. Walter had asked much the same question of Dr Feldman. The doctor had surprised him with one of his textbook responses.

'Tell me about that,' he'd said.

Dr Feldman often did this, said things that were just so cliché psychiatrist that Walter looked at him out of the corner of his eye and suspected him of taking the piss—but apparently he wasn't.

'Well, we all look much the same, we all behave much the same, don't we?' Walter had said. 'I mean, I'm talking fairly generally now. We're all polite. We all nod and say 'hi' and talk about our jobs and our kids, if we've got any, or the property market, or the Wintergardens palm tree that keeps dying, but they don't know me. They don't know anything about me really.'

'I suppose not,' Dr Feldman said. 'But it's true the other way also, isn't it? You don't know them.'

'I guess not.'

'Everyone's got something else going on don't you think, other than what we see? Things they don't necessarily share. Perhaps something they hide, their most shameful secret, or the moment they are privately most proud of. What if we knew that something, that secret, instantly, as soon as we met everyone?'

'Mmm,' Walter said noncommittally.

'What if everyone walked around wearing their secret on their neck, like a big fat goitre the size of a football. Imagine if we could see that, see that one thing, hmm? Imagine that.'

'Yes. Well, I suppose that would be … odd.' Walter stopped for a minute, pretending to contemplate what the doctor had just told him. 'And then what?'

'Well then, Walter, you'd realise that everyone has something, including you, and that this in itself doesn't make you better or worse, or in fact special or different.'

'OK,' Walter nodded. 'So what are you telling me?'

'Well, nothing. I'm not telling you anything.'

'I mean, what am I meant to do? About the goitre thing? Should I … do you think I should ask people to tell me their innermost secrets?' Walter wasn't convinced. It didn't sound like the sort of thing he would do at all.

'No no. No.' Dr Feldman took a breath. 'You don't need to ask anyone anything. But if you just keep in mind that the people around you are not … you know, there's more to them than meets the eye. You don't know anything about anyone by travelling to work with them on the Lilydale Express of a morning, that's what I'm saying, Walter.'

'I take the Wintergardens express.'

'U-huh.' Dr Feldman took his glasses off and massaged the bridge of his nose. 'Whichever.'

'Lilydale's a whole other line,' Walter said. 'Other side of town.'

'Exactly,' Dr Feldman said. 'Good point.'

*

As much as Walter hated to admit it, Dr Feldman had a good point. Even though his neighbours, all those husbands and wives, seemed to Walter to be cut from the same cloth, if he thought about them properly, they were in actual fact quite a mixed bunch. Maggie was, certainly, a bit more artsy than the rest with her pale skin and her little neck-scarf knotted at the side. Missy, well, she stood out for other reasons. Even culturally they were a hotchpotch now he came to think about it. Graeme had Spanish blood in there somewhere, he seemed to remember. And Eddie's real name was something Russian, even though he sported a number of traditional Maori tattoos. Then there was Colin's second wife. She was born in Hong Kong and had taken Elvie as an anglicised name because she absolutely adored Elvis Presley—not so much for his music as his movies. In fact, now that he thought about it, Elvie looked like an Asian Ann-Margret—all hair and pedal-pushers.

They weren't quite so ordinary underneath either. Just as Doctor Feldman had suggested, they all had their special little party-trick or oddity which, when Walter gave himself a moment to think about it, had become common knowledge.

Eddie, for example, had confessed over beers in someone's shed at some long-past event that he had a double hole in the nob of his penis and when he ejaculated he spurted in two distinct directions. This had caused much comment amongst the other men present. He had gone on to tell them how, as a young man, it had been the dream of his life to be featured in a porn film, but as he didn't quite know how to go about making this happen, it didn't. Egged on further he admitted that when he had first started going out with Jenny, she had been impressed with his dual ejaculations and during their younger, headier, more down-and-dirty sexual exploits, he had been allowed to come on her tits, both at once and quite separately. More recently, after the twins, it had been decided that his dick should be consigned to a condom, from within which, Eddie told them with a slouch in his shoulders, a double-ejaculation meant very little.

Colin's second wife Elvie had also revealed to Maggie, and Maggie had told Walter, that Colin only had nine toes. The big toe on his right foot had been severed by a lawn mower when he was a teenager—he was mowing the lawn in thongs, which apparently hadn't seemed all that dangerous back in the 70s. He was rushed to hospital with his father while his mother scoured their backyard for the tip of his toe in case the doctors were able to do something about sewing it back on. She was, however, unable to find it, and Colin had nightmares for years afterwards that their dog, a small and very jumpy fox-terrier called Cazaly had found and eaten it. In his adult years Colin found himself unable to become a policeman, which had been his boyhood dream, refused to get a puppy for either of the children of his first marriage when they were kids, and most recently had contracted a gardening firm to mow his lawns, something no-one in the mostly garden-proud Wintergardens understood in the slightest.

There were many other examples that Walter, if pressed, could probably remember. Even so, as different as his neighbours all were, as many oddities as they had, they were similar in that Walter felt distant from them, from their easy, smiling facades and neighbourly chitchat. They were to him, every last one of them, something that he wasn't, and he didn't know how else to say it.

*

'Do you think it's been long enough?' Graeme asked. He was standing at the BBQ talking with Eddie—the two alpha males of the group. Walter was standing a little way away from them, picking through a plate of salad with a fork. They obviously didn't think he could hear, but their voices carried. He realised by the direction Graeme gestured with the tongs that they were talking about Missy who was across the other side of the terrace with some of the other women.

'What's the statute of limitations with something like that?' Graeme continued.

'Statute of limitations!' Eddie gave a single snort of derision that doubled as a laugh, acknowledging that it was a good joke without actually finding it amusing enough to laugh.

'She's gotta be gagging for it by now,' Graeme said, flipping a burger on the barbeque.

'She'd have to be to give you a chance,' Eddie said.

Walter closed his eyes for a second. It was just like those dickheads at work and their inconsequential conversations which were nothing more than a string of meaningless non sequiturs.

When he opened his eyes he found that Missy was in front of him.

She looked around all of the men, wavered a moment on Eddie as the youngest and strongest, but moved on to Walter.

'Walter, could you give me a hand for a minute?'

Walter blushed scarlet and the rest of the guys passed around knowing looks. He opened his mouth and tried to talk, to ask Missy what she wanted but there was a bit of something, something from the salad he'd been eating sitting there in his throat like a butter menthol or something, like a big knob of something or other that just wouldn't go down, like a ... He clapped eyes on her nipples and stared for a moment before looking away. He swallowed, but still the obstruction in his throat refused to move. In his head all he could see were those nipples, big and round like butter menthols.

'Walter, are you right mate?' That was Eddie, smart-arse all over his tone.

'Sorry,' Walter croaked. 'Sorry. Stuck in throat.'

As he moved away inside, someone, one of the blokes standing around the barbeque, stifled a laugh.

*

Between the kitchen where he gulped down a glass of water to clear his throat and returning to the deck where the others were gathered, Walter found himself in a passageway, cool and carpeted, slightly dim after the bright outdoors. He stopped for a second and had a moment to himself, a moment between the kitchen and the deck, the sink and the barbeque, solitude and the group.

He knew they all had their own party trick, their own fifteen minutes of fame, their own guilty secret, they all had something they felt defined them, one little coin they worried away at with their thumb, in secret, in their pocket, around and around, until it was shiny with too much handling—but in a flash of perspective he wondered if perhaps he felt different to them because his own particular defining characteristic was known and understood by everyone but him.

He left the relative silence of the passageway and continued out onto the deck to join the others.

*

A little later in the afternoon the conversation turned to the stabbing incident on the train. Walter momentarily forgot his agitation and listened in. It appeared that Eddie had actually been on the train in which the stabbing had occurred.

'So you were in the actual carriage?' Graeme asked him.

'Nah, not the one it happened in. The next one.'

'But you saw it?'

'Well, not really. You know what it's like in the mornings—squashed in like sardines—but in the next carriage along they were going berserk, squashing right back towards the windows at the end near us. They crowded in through the door, but they couldn't move very far in, because we were packed in tight. There was a whole lot of talk then and we got an idea of what was going on. They were talking about a man with a knife, although it wasn't really clear what was going on. And they kept yelling for us to move further into the carriage, which no-one really did. You know how it is.'

'And when you got to North Melbourne?'

'A whole heap of us got out of the train. There were people everywhere. Two or three carriages emptied almost completely. There was still a lot of confusion about what had happened. I saw one guy with blood on his arm, on his sleeve, you know? Not good. But nah, I didn't see the actual guy.'

'Drugs I suppose,' Jenny said.

'Isn't it always?' another of them said.

'To be trapped like that, on an express train with a crack-head with a knife.'

'It's hard enough being on an express during peak hour at the best of times.'

At that moment Graeme realised that Helen had been making subtle but stern head-shaking movements at him, and, with a quick glance at Missy, then Walter, he changed the topic and the conversation skewed off onto the topic of the Wintergardens palm trees.

Walter, who hadn't noticed Helen's head-shaking or the rapid conversational left-turn, found himself beside Eddie, the two of them suddenly and unexpectedly side-lined.

'Which carriage was it?' Walter asked him, quietly, alongside the new conversation.

'Sorry?' Eddie smiled at him. He looked tough, but he was a nice guy.

'Which carriage did it happen on?'

'The next carriage along from mine.'

'Yes, yes, you said that. Towards the city? Or away from it?'

'Towards the city. Yeah, in front of us.'

'And which carriage were you on?'

'Sorry?'

'The third, the fourth? The end carriage?'

'Dunno, mate. Don't know exactly. In the middle somewhere.'

'Well, where do you get on?'

'Wintergardens. Same as you.'

'No, I mean, where do you stand on the station? Where do you get in the train?'

'I stand in the middle of the shelter most mornings. That puts me at the right spot for the exit the other end.'

'That would be,' Walter gave it a moment's thought. 'That would be the fourth carriage of the train, then?'

'If you say so, mate.'

The fourth carriage of the train, and he, Walter, usually got on the third carriage of the train, one carriage closer to the city than Eddie, and the carriage, according to his story, where the man with the knife had been.

'Thanks,' Walter said to Eddie, and just as he said it he realised that Maggie was looking at him from across the deck. She looked either suspicious or concerned, or perhaps both. He couldn't be sure. She wasn't that far away and he wondered if she had heard him asking Eddie all those questions about the train. On the other hand, why shouldn't she listen? And if she had been listening and had overheard what he was saying, why would that make any difference to her?

Across the terrace Maggie turned her head back to the conversation happening around her.

*

Michael Everaardt remembered very well the first time he'd seen Maggie Kovak. He'd been hanging out with some colleagues out the front of the hospital, waiting for a statement perhaps from the doctors, or the police, waiting for a glimpse of Walter Kovak, if there was one to be had, or alternatively a glimpse of someone visiting him, which was more probable although not perhaps as much of a scoop—this wife of his, maybe?

When she did arrive, Michael was impressed, as he felt vaguely he was meant to be. A dark car pulled up out the very front of the hospital in that sort of expectant way that barely rolling expensive cars did, presumably so she could exit the car and launch straight up the stairs and past the congregation of photographers and journalists. In actual fact, of course, the crawling dark-windowed car attracted so much attention that all it really achieved was that every eye was turned her way when she got out. So it was that Michael, along with the rest of them saw the back door of the car open and a pair of stockinged legs, nice legs, shapely, long, feet clad in neat little high-heeled shoes, swing into view as if the woman was swivelling on her bum, knees together, adhering perhaps to some forgotten law of etiquette.

She had stalked through them, up the stairs and inside before he'd really had a chance to recover from the leg-swivelling. She was certainly a piece of work, he'd give her that. Good looking, slender and stylish. She wore a short women's trench-coat, tied off tightly at her waist, with only a suggestion of black hemline underneath. Her face was pale, her lips red and her eyes hidden by sunglasses.

He had wondered at the time how old she might be. Too old, he thought, for him. But how old was too old? The whole cougar thing was making it much more acceptable these days to bag older women. He'd always had a thing for them anyhow, which was kind of lucky.

She had certainly sounded older on the phone when he had spoken to her the day after his quickly abandoned visit to Walter Kovak at Equity Insurance. Maybe not older as such, but certainly there was something mature about the way she spoke, slower maybe, her words a bit more carefully pronounced. There was something a little Mrs Robinson about it. He could imagine her saying the line too: 'I am not trying to seduce you … would you like me to seduce you? Is that what you're trying to tell me?' His answer, of course, would be yes.

He was surprised actually that she hadn't hung up in his ear.

'Yes,' she had said in her phone-answering Mrs Robinson voice after he had introduced himself. 'What can I do for you?'

He said that he would like to meet up with her. He wasn't going to chance lengthy explanations over the phone.

'Have you approached my husband already?'

He couldn't really deny it. He told her that yes, he had and that her husband was not interested in participating.

'I could have told you you'd get nowhere with Walter.'

Michael decided not to go down that path. Not yet anyway. Was there a suggestion of discord in those few words? Instead he returned to his suggestion that they should meet up to discuss a possible profile piece.

After a moment Maggie said: 'I don't see why not.'

Michael felt his gut clench.

That was a yes!

Then she'd given him a time and a place and he'd quickly agreed, with the phone hoiked up between his shoulder and his cheek as he wrote down the address and the time and date on the margin of a newspaper. She had not been keen on the idea of him coming to her home—one of those new suburbs on the outskirts of the north-west of Melbourne, something-gardens. Michael didn't mind that in the slightest—he hadn't ventured out to those new suburbs and he wasn't at all keen to. They had instead agreed to meet up the following day at a café down the road from where she worked, which suited Michael fine—he was an inner city kinda lad.

He hung up the phone and stared at what he'd written, wondering if he'd really had the conversation at all. It seemed so incongruous, so easy—too easy, he thought, especially given the reaction he had received from Walter in the office. Here, he thought, was whatever the opposite of a united front was—a divided front that would be. Then there was the fact that they had both, she and her husband, avoided the press ever since the accident. So why had she said yes? Why now? Why him? He felt keyed up, and slightly edgy, as if he needed to be nimble-witted and clever so as not to fuck up this opportunity. Which was a shit, he thought, given that nimble-witted and clever were not words that even his mother would honestly use to describe him—he usually got by on charm and an easy, slightly-too-familiar manner. But whatever—he'd got his foot in the door. He'd work the rest out later.

He popped the top off a beer and raised it to the phone.

'Here's to you, Mrs Robinson.'

7.
WATCH OUT FOR EIGHT FORTY-FIVE

It wasn't that Walter was a clock-watcher as such, with all that the term implied—he felt he had a sound work ethic—but he did keep an eye on the time, which in his view wasn't the same thing at all. Punctuality was important to him. So on an ordinary, regular kind of day at the office, Walter would pack up and leave on the stroke of 5.00pm, and if everything went well, in his favour, if everything clicked into place, he would make the 5.08pm express from Flagstaff Station to Wintergardens.

For Walter it was a challenge he set himself, catching that particular train, a little game he played with himself, just inside his own head. It wasn't anything to do with actually needing to be on the 5.08 train. That wasn't the important thing at all. If that was the only purpose of the challenge, he could easily be on the 5.08pm train—if he left work early for example, or ran like a mad thing through the streets to the station. But it wasn't important that he was on the train, as such, it was just important that he catch it in his own way, by his own rules.

To begin with he wasn't allowed to leave work until the clock on the wall ticked over to 5pm exactly. Then, of course, having done his hours, he was officially free to go. So he would calmly log off his computer, collect his coat and briefcase, walk to the foyer and press the lift-call button. There was no hurry about it, there was no rushing around, no frenzied pushing and re-pushing of the lift button. He would simply walk through Reception in a measured way, say goodnight to Ros-at-Reception, as he did every night, and press the lift button, once and once only. He wouldn't linger, certainly, but neither did he rush.

If anything transpired to delay him, if someone came up to his desk for example and asked him something just before 5pm, well of course the game was over, he would never make the 5.08 express. Likewise if the lifts took ages, as they sometimes did, or they were completely full and he had to let a couple of lifts go without him, wait until there was a lift with room in it before he could squeeze himself in, then again there was no way he was going to make his train. But if all went to plan, if he got out of work without being waylaid by a colleague at his desk or in the foyer, and if the lift arrived promptly and wasn't packed, and he got in and went straight down to the foyer and out into the street, if all that happened, then he might, he just might make it.

From his building to the Flagstaff train station was a matter of a block and a half through two sets of pedestrian crossing lights. Of course running was out of the question, against the rules. Walter didn't run for trains. He simply wasn't the type to run through the street, and anyway, it wasn't, in his head, part of the game, it wasn't allowed. He was allowed, of course, to walk briskly, it made sense to walk briskly if you wanted to catch a train. He never dawdled, but likewise he never ran.

If all had gone well to that point, and the two pedestrian crossing lights had been in his favour, Walter would get a prickle of excitement, because that's when it started to get interesting. If he'd made it that far, there was a good chance he would make the train.

Then, though, came the tricky bit. How many people would there be at the barriers to the station? If there were no crowds, no lines, if he got through almost immediately, and there was no hold-up, no trouble about his pass not scanning, and if the two sets of escalators to his platform weren't clogged with people who didn't keep to the left, a pet peeve of his, and he could therefore walk down the moving escalators, and if the train was actually there, if it was on time and came into the station at 5.08 as timetabled, then Walter might be able to step on the train, not having run or hurried, not having left work early, he might be able to simply step on the train just at the very moment before the warning beeps began and the doors closed at his back.

If it all happened like that, if it all came together, as, to be truthful, it rarely did, for the odds of all of those variables happening in Walter's favour, one after the other weren't good—he'd done the calculations—but if they did come together and he stepped onto that train just in time, he felt a little thrill of … was it triumph? Pleasure? Wellbeing? He felt as though the world through which he stalked, usually so messy and irregular, that world, just for eight minutes, had been on his side.

*

The Monday after the barbeque, Walter purchased his usual lunch, but this time he didn't go to his bench in the churchyard nearby. This time he returned to the office and ate at his desk, using the time to check the online news pages to see if there were any updates on the story of the stabbing on the train.

He found one or two. There were new eye-witness accounts, stories gleaned from those in the carriage, those on the platform, those injured in the incident. There was certainly no lack of witnesses willing to comment on what they had seen. Some of the articles came with photographs of the witnesses, or those injured. The name of the man who had been taken to hospital where he had later died had also now been released, a man called Frank Bell. He worked at one of the big banks, although which one remained unnamed for some reason. The photo of him showed a jowly man with grey hair and glasses, mild and ordinary, but not perhaps as old as he looked.

There were no new details about the man with the knife. His identity had been established, but was withheld from the reports. There was a picture of him, his face pixilated for publication, a still from CCTV footage, presumably from the North Melbourne station, where he had been forced from the train by a number of commuters.

Walter studied the picture carefully. The youth was wearing skinny-leg denims, an oversized sloppy windcheater and, possibly, although it was difficult to tell with the pixilation, a baseball cap. About five male commuters held him by the arms and wrists, and one, it seemed, by the back of the trousers. These men, those who overpowered him and dragged him from the train, were in stark contrast all wearing corporate attire. There was something disturbing about the picture, Walter thought. Perhaps it was the flapping of all those ties, those suit jackets. It made him think of seagulls swooping around fighting over a discarded chip.

Walter wondered how old the pixilated man was. He seemed young, very young. Was that why his name had been withheld, because of his age? How old was he? 16? Younger? However youthful he had been, he had certainly been a danger, had stabbed a man, more than one person, although according to these new reports some of the injuries sustained by commuters were not directly from the youth and his knife but due to the press of commuters in the train. People had fallen in the panic. Even so, looking at that picture Walter felt the kid was menaced more than menacing.

He wondered where the man who was stabbed, this Frank man, had been when this photo was captured by CCTV. He didn't seem to be one of the men manhandling the kid onto the platform. They were all a lot more lithe than Frank Bell had appeared in his photo in the paper. Was he back in the carriage, lying there stabbed and bleeding? He didn't die at the scene, Walter remembered, but later in hospital, so he might not, at the time this photo was captured, have been lying flat out with blood all over him. He might, in fact, have been standing amongst the rest of them there in the background, not even realising he had been stabbed, perhaps just feeling a pain in his side, which he might have taken to be the excitement, the exertion, or a pre-existing heart condition. And moments after this photo had been taken, he might have put his hand to his side, or wherever the wound had been, and notice, taking his hand away, that there was blood.

Walter was no good with blood. No good at all. Other people's certainly, but especially his own. He was glad it hadn't been him who had been stabbed and bleeding—a silly thing to think perhaps, but that's what popped into his head—and it could quite possibly have been him if things had gone a little differently that morning.

At this point in his thoughts Walter noticed in the still from the CCTV footage a man standing a little way away from the main group, standing in the background amongst other commuters. His head was cut off, but there he was, from the shoulders down, tall and thin, wearing a grey suit and a red tie, just like the man who had spoken to him that morning on the platform, the morning of this incident on the train.

*

That afternoon something happened to throw Walter even further off track. He had come out to see Ros-at-Reception about a courier delivery he was waiting on and while she was on the phone about it he noticed that, behind her little counter, she had a half-completed Sudoku puzzle. She wasn't apparently all that good at Sudoku, as she had pencilled in and rubbed out a few different numbers and had missed some really easy ones. He idly looked over the puzzle, mentally working through a few more numbers that she had missed.

It was in the middle of this innocuous over-the-shoulder Sudoku moment that Walter got a jolt. He saw vividly in his mind a woman doing a Sudoku puzzle—not Ros-at-Reception, another woman at another time and in another place. She was quite a large woman with too-large, square-ish glasses with the arms connected towards the bottom, perched right down at the very tip of her nose. She had a newspaper folded back on itself on her lap and was filling in number after number quite rapidly.

It was an innocent enough flashback to the moments just before the accident, and it certainly wasn't the first flashback he had ever had, but they always came so unexpectedly that even though they were quite ordinary they filled him with a sense of dread completely out of proportion.

He went back to his desk, walking like a zombie, plonked down in his chair, keyed in his password to unlock his computer and sat there for a moment staring at the screen. His email was open. His wrists rested on the desk, his fingers hovered over his keyboard as though he was going to begin typing, but he didn't begin typing, he just stared at the screen and Outlook was reflected on the surface of his eyes.

After some time he blinked and his eyes moved to the clock, focussed there for a moment, registered the time. Amazingly it was just a minute or so before 5.00pm. He thought distantly of the 5.08pm Wintergardens. Perhaps tonight would be his lucky night.

He waited out the minute, watched the second hand tick up, past the ten and the eleven, and the moment it passed the twelve and the time was officially 5.00pm, Walter clicked on the mouse to shut down his computer. He put his wallet, newly purchased on the weekend, in his briefcase, got up, put his coat over his arm, pushed his chair in under his desk and walked off into the foyer as his computer hummed, clicked and closed down behind him. There had been no phone calls on the brink of 5.00pm, no colleague had come to his desk to distract him, and when he got to the foyer, there was no-one there waiting for the lifts. So far, he thought, still rather blankly, so good.

'Goodnight Ros,' he said to Ros-at-Reception.

'Goodnight,' she said, with her end-of-the-day downward inflection. Good mornings required a keyed up tone, as if acknowledging the promise the day held, whereas goodnights were more subdued, indicating the weight of a full day of hard work and the promise of home and hearth.

Walter pushed the lift-call button and a lift came almost immediately, which he felt sure was another good sign. When the doors opened there was someone else in there, a man, but Walter took little notice of him. He stepped in and saw that the G button was already lit up. The lift doors closed and the lift began to descend. Walter and the man stood side by side, facing front, in the usual manner, looking at the numbers lighting up as they counted down the floors. They were lighting up with agreeable regularity, one after the other, quite speedily, and the lift appeared to be whistling directly down without any other stops. Amazingly it appeared no-one else in the building was, at that moment, requiring the lift. They might, Walter thought, even make it all the way to the ground floor without any other stops. At this rate, the 5.08pm was looking better and better. He began to perk up a little.

It was at this moment that the other man spoke.

'Not stopping all stations for a change,' he said.

What?

Walter turned to look at him. He was a regular looking man, mild, with a bald head, clipped close, and black plastic rimmed glasses, quite old fashioned, of the type worn by artsy people in the sort of suburb Maggie's boutique was in. He wore a navy suit and a gold tie with little brown things on it that looked, remarkably, like little acorns or pineapples. He smiled at Walter, displaying a mouth slightly too full of teeth.

Walter ignored him and turned back to watch the numbers light up, as they inevitably did, counting down the floors one by one. So it was that he was watching the numbers, not the man next to him, so he didn't see him say it, he didn't actually see his lips move, but he heard him say it, loud and clear, right in his ear. He definitely heard him say it.

Watch out for eight forty-five.

'Eight forty what?' Walter spun back to him. 'What did you say?'

The man smiled with slightly less teeth.

'Sorry?'

'What did you just say?'

'About stopping all stations?' He looked nonplussed.

'No, not that. Eight forty-five? What does that mean?'

The man shook his head. He appeared bewildered.

'I don't know what you're ...' But before Walter could finish his sentence the lift doors opened with a ding and the other man stepped around him and out of the lift.

'Who are you?' Walter called after him, but the lift doors started closing and he had to jam his briefcase in between them and jab at the door-open button. When the doors did slide open again, there was no sign of the bald man in the navy suit.

*

Walter didn't make the 5.08pm express from Flagstaff station to Wintergardens that night. He walked to the station, still bouncy on his innersoles, sure, but it was a slow amble, not the sort of brisk walk he was likely to catch a train with. On the escalators down into Flagstaff he was stuck behind people standing stationary on the right hand side, but he didn't notice this, didn't even scoff and click his tongue at them. He arrived at the platform and stepped onto the next train to come in, whatever it was. He had been so jolted by the incident in the lift that he was completely unaware of what time the train was meant to be there or what time it in fact was, and it needed a pretty good jolt to render Walter unaware of the time.

In his head he was doing it again.

Imagine your discomfort. Do you see it?

'Yes,' he nodded.

Would you like to get rid of it?

'Yes,' he nodded.

Then imagine screwing it up into a little ball.

His right hand made a fist.

And throwing it away.

His right hand made a muted throwing gesture.

That man in the lift, though! Who was that man in the lift? Who was he, and why would he talk to Walter like that? He'd never seen him in the lifts before and he didn't know him from a bar of soap. How dare he just speak to him like that, right there in the lift? And to say something so random and then deny having said anything—it was stupid, stupid.

Getting blustery and a little annoyed, if only in his head, Walter felt the best thing to do would be to ignore it completely. He could do that. Or could he?

Imagine screwing it up into a little ball and throwing it away.

He could ignore it—maybe he could ignore it—if it weren't for the warning of the man on the train station platform. *Don't get on the next train.* He hadn't, and that next train had subsequently been the site of violence in which a number of people were injured and a man called Frank Bell had afterwards died. He had heeded that warning, OK, mostly because he was so rattled about the circumstances of it, the unfortunate coincidence that made the subject of trains such a raw one for him, but in any case he had heeded that warning and not boarded the train. And OK, sure, again, there was nothing to say that if he had been on the train, he would have been stabbed, but perhaps he would have been. Perhaps. How could he know that? And so, knowing that, or not knowing that as the case may be, how could he now possibly ignore the man in the lift and this second apparently illogical warning?

What could eight forty-five mean though? Was it another train? Was it an 8.45 train he was being warned against now? It could be.

But he rarely travelled at that time. He was usually at work right on 8.00am, rarely so late to be still leaving Wintergardens at only 8.45am. Likewise he rarely travelled home from the city as late as 8.45pm, and like many others he travelled everywhere by car on the weekends and at any other time outside the regular workday week commute.

Walter scoffed at himself. This was all beside the point. How could this man, or the man the other day, how could anyone possibly have any sort of pre-knowledge of anything that was going to happen to him or anyone else? Walter just plain didn't believe in that kind of premonition. He didn't believe in fortune telling or intuition or star signs, those sorts of things. Sure, he was aware that he was lumping a whole lot of possibly unrelated stuff together, but in his mind they were the same kinds of things and he didn't believe, as it were, in that sort of belief. He believed in facts, facts and figures and things he could hear and see and smell and put on an Excel spreadsheet. There were reasons that things happened, and everything could, one way or another, be explained away rationally and scientifically. That was the way the world worked.

The warning from the man on the train station, for example, could be put aside as a mere erratic and unusual occurrence. Why, Walter could think of a number of explanations. Perhaps the man was delusional or mad, uttering cryptic warnings all the time. The stabbing that occurred later that morning could have been nothing to do with the man's warning whatsoever, it could have been a mere coincidence. Or, perhaps the man had foreknowledge of what was going to happen on the train because he knew an unstable young man with a knife was on the train. Perhaps he knew, or suspected, or feared that there was going to be some incident on the train. Perhaps he was in some way connected to the kid who had done it, perhaps he was trying to find him and stop him from doing something he had threatened to do. That sort of prior knowledge Walter could believe in. It would fit. It could fit.

He could believe in either of those explanations for the first warning easily, if only it weren't for the man in the lift. Two apparently random, cryptic warnings by two separate strangers? That he couldn't dismiss, couldn't explain away as coincidence. That, to him, was like a brick wall. Something else was going on here. Not something about premonition or precognition or anything hokey like that, Walter thought sternly. No, there was something human and tangible and definite going on, there had to be, and that meant, it logically must mean, that there was someone behind these two strangers and their warnings. But who? And why would someone do that to him?

Perhaps, he thought, struggling to find an explanation, it was some sort of joke. His mind snapped to those two jokers from the office, Mick and David, the new guy. They'd come up to him the other day and made that stupid teasing joke about autoerotic strangulation, then he'd moments later heard them giggling and snuffling over in the kitchenette. He hated those two guys, he hated their type, because they were bullies, but also because they were regular everyday idiots who would with the minimum effort and smarts get ahead. The world, such as it was, belonged to dickheads like these two. Could they be behind the warnings? But why? Why? Surely they wouldn't be doing something so intricate and involved just for a bit of fun. Would they? Their jokes up to now had been so coarse, so unsubtle, and usually just about unnerving him with the mention of something sexual or slightly dirty.

Walter realised that his shoulders were bunched up and his back was painful from sitting so rigidly, that his face was clammy and damp around the edges of his hair and in his collar. He also noticed that a woman sitting across from him was looking at him strangely, as if she was going to ask if he was feeling alright.

With a jolt of embarrassment Walter relaxed his shoulders, wiped the blade of his first finger across his forehead like a squeegee, made a nervous I'm-OK-thanks kind of smile at the Good Samaritan woman and turned to look out the window. He had a horror of acting conspicuously in public, and that's exactly what he must have been doing—walking like a zombie, sweating and staring blankly while his mind reeled. Oh God, perhaps he had been muttering to himself. He hoped he hadn't been muttering to himself.

For a second he thought he had it. What if this was why they were doing it—Mick and David, or someone else, whoever—to get at him, for the fun of seeing him jittery and sweating and confused, for the fun of getting under his skin, messing with him? Walter Kovak, the freak who wasn't like them. They would like that, watching him fall apart. That would appeal, wouldn't it?

He didn't quite believe in this solution even as it occurred to him, but it appealed to him, to the victim in him, the schoolboy he had been. He'd like to see those two on the end of a joke like this. He'd like to see their stupid faces. He'd like to see them hurt and remorseful.

Eight forty-five, though, what was that all about? Because it must have some meaning, some significance.

*

When Walter got home the house was empty. He put his briefcase and his coat down in the hall and went through to the kitchen.

'Maggie?'

There was a note on the fridge under a magnet, informing him that she was out for the night with her mother. Walter felt a sense of relief—as long as Arlette wasn't coming there he didn't mind very much what was going on. He glanced at the stovetop and in the oven, but there was no sign of any dinner. He was, not unexpectedly, supposed to fend for himself. He opened the freezer and pulled out at random one of the many Tupperware containers in there with sauces and casseroles and soups. Maggie was a great one for making extra and freezing things. She was, in fact, a good cook, although she no longer took as much trouble over dinner if it was just she and Walter eating.

'It's just us,' she would say. 'Why bother?'

In the early days of their marriage she had bothered.

It's this house, Walter thought. Not that he believed the house was unlucky. Of course not. He did, though, believe the house in Wintergardens had come to represent what their marriage had become, perhaps because whatever had happened, the degeneration, had happened there, since they moved in.

Things just weren't the same, not like the earlier days, in their flat in the inner city. Maggie's flat, it had been, and Walter had moved in. They had been happy there, eating together, cooking together. Well, Maggie would cook. She would prepare meals for them, experimenting with new recipes. She would get Walter to chop things, or just sit there and talk to her while she cooked. Walter had very much appreciated it. He was sure he had let her know how much he appreciated it—the food and the cooking of it.

Now? Maggie was out with her mother doing who-knew-what and he, Walter, was at home, sorting through bricks of frozen sauces and soups for something to microwave for dinner, in a dim house where they never cooked together any more, and which was too big for them.

Too big, he thought. *And too empty.*

*

Before dinner he set out for a walk to clear his head. It was just before sunset and the light was strong and golden, but would fade rapidly before too long, he knew, in the manner of an autumn sunset in Melbourne.

There were two types of people out on the streets of Wintergardens at that time of night—those exercising and those exercising their dogs. Walter wasn't a jogger and he didn't have a dog. He really felt the lack of a black Labrador that night, but it felt good to hit the footpath, get out of that empty house.

There were three types of houses in Wintergardens, three designs which differed only slightly from their fellows, and they repeated themselves in sequence time after time as Walter walked block after block. So similar were they that after turning a corner or two he began to feel slightly disoriented.

A man and woman rounded the corner and came towards him. They were an older couple with matching running shoes, running skins, fitted zipped-up Kathmandu tops and scrawny-fit bodies. They looked peaky and perked-up and had the air about them of being determined to get a good walk in. They had the rolling gait and the bent piston-arms of power-walkers, and as they moved past him, one either side, with a curt nod and a murmured 'good evening', Walter got an unexpected jolt of recognition—that was the man who had spoken to him on the train station.

He stopped in his tracks and turned, watched them power-walking away with their rumps waggling in time.

Was it him or wasn't it? It had been so quick a glimpse it was hard to tell. He was of the same type, had the same colouring, was the same age, and he certainly seemed familiar, but Walter wasn't sure whether that was just because he was a familiar type—clean shaven, mild eyes, regular features, salt-and-pepper hair. The voice now, it wasn't even as though Walter could remember the voice enough to know if it was him or not. He remembered what the man had said well enough, without really remembering the voice. It was, again, a plain, regular voice, polite, without an accent. Remarkably, the more Walter thought about the man on the station, about what he looked and sounded like, the more he found he couldn't really remember much about him at all. He was just so ordinary. He was more of a type of man than an actual man.

Walter was reminded of that painting by Magritte of a man wearing a suit and tie and a bowler hat, but where his face should have been was a giant green apple.

If only he had a photo of the man at the platform, then he could remind himself what he looked like. But how to get a photo from that day?

Remembering the photo he'd seen online earlier that day Walter considered for a moment trying to get hold of CCTV footage from his station. He tried to remember if there were cameras at the Wintergardens station, but couldn't. Would they have kept images from so long ago? And in any case, how did a member of the public, Mr Joe Average, a man like him, go about getting hold of CCTV footage? He was sure it wasn't the sort of thing they usually made available to the public. He did wonder, though, what he'd see if he did get it? He wondered if he'd see himself, viewed from slightly above, grainy and mugshot-pallid, blank eyed, with his feet planted, moving backwards and forwards like a praying mantis. He gave a shiver of remembered embarrassment.

*

A little later Walter was back at home and in his study, and again reaching for that small volume outlining the odds of dying. He flicked through the book until he came to the page he wanted, found the statistics he needed, and copied them down onto a pad on his desk. From there he went through careful and accurate calculations, and worked out that the odds of a man of his age and location dying from assault by a sharp object were one in one thousand eight hundred and ninety three. He wrote this in his little pocket diary, on the same page as he had scribbled other odds, then hesitated as he caught sight of the clock. It was almost 8.45pm.

Even if he didn't believe in the warning as a warning as such, it still must mean something, quite academically and within the context of the fiction it undoubtedly was, there must still be a meaning. He wondered what it was.

He sat quite still, his hands folded on the desk, and as the second hand ticked past the 12 and it was officially 8.45pm—absolutely nothing happened. He did not move until the second hand had ticked all the way around the face of the clock. He sat and listened during that time, and all he heard was the tick of the clock and the far off murmur of a car on the street passing by. Then it was 8.46pm and he smiled at himself, more amused than ashamed of his nonsense.

Of course nothing had happened. What had he expected?

*

Walter went to bed relatively early, but couldn't sleep. He heard the car in the drive at just past 11.00pm. Maggie was home. He rolled over away from the door and pretended to be asleep. He thought it highly probable that when he finally got to sleep he would have the dream again. Sure enough, he did.

*

'Are they always the same?' Dr Feldman had asked him in an early session.

'Mostly the same, yes,' Walter had said. He had known this was coming, this particular conversation, this particular discussion. He'd known because Dr Feldman had told him it was important for him to talk about his dream, describe it. It was an important part of the process, he was told. Dr Feldman had encouraged him to come around to it in his own time, without pressure, when he was ready, and eventually he got to it, agreed to it, came along to one of his sessions prepared to describe the dream.

It wasn't easy, though. He felt a sense of shame and immaturity about the situation—it seemed to him childish to be having nightmares at all, let alone be in a position where he was expected to describe them to someone else.

Dr Feldman told him to close his eyes.

'OK,' Walter said, unnecessarily. 'They're closed.'

'How do they start?' Dr Feldman asked from the other side of his closed eyes. He sounded quite close. Walter took a breath—exhaled it in an OK-lets-get-this-over-with kind of way.

'Well it's dark.'

'Mmm,' Dr Feldman murmured.

'They begin with dark. Just ... blackness. I can't see anything, but I start to realise it's not just, well, you know, it's not just that I'm asleep or lying in bed in a dark room. No. I realise I'm in a train.'

Dr Feldman didn't say anything so after a moment Walter continued.

'I know because I start hearing that noise they make, sort of galloping, and the ground feels unsteady underneath me, like I'm on a train, in a carriage and it's swaying. It feels like that, but that doesn't seem quite right, because I'm *not* on a train. I know that. I don't know how I know, I mean, there isn't anything that I can see, it's all dark, totally pitch black, but I just know, like you do in a dream—I know I'm not on a train.'

'Keep going,' the doctor said.

'There's a smell ... a sort of old-dirt smell, you know, like earth that's gone off? And something else, something that's ... I don't know. Blood? The smell of blood? I don't know what blood smells like, not really. I don't know. But in the dream, it's like I do know, and I know it's a lot of blood.' Walter opened his eyes. 'You know?'

'Eyes.'

Walter closed his eyes. He sighed again. Kept going.

'All this time I can't see anything. It's pitch black and I'm petrified. Frozen to the spot. It's like I can't move. I can't chance it. I don't know if there's a … a cliff edge in front of me, or a wall. I don't really know if I'm standing up or kneeling, or hanging upside down. I can't tell. I have no idea where I am. I'm just in the dark and totally disoriented. But after a while … I mean, gradually, I become aware … absolutely positive actually, that there's something else with me there in the dark. Something just beside me, or in front of me, somewhere very close to me in the dark. Like, maybe it's moving around me, from side to side, right in my face, or behind my back. I become positive that I see movement in the darkness, a flash of something like light reflected in the surface of an eye, or I feel a breath on my face or something brush against my hand.' Walter opened his eyes. 'You know?'

'Eyes closed.'

Walter closed his eyes. He made a small noise and kept going.

'I'm … I'm terrified. I feel … like I have to get away, escape … but at the same time I know that if I keep completely still, if I slow my breathing … whatever it is won't notice me … it doesn't matter, actually, what it is … I know that something horrible is just behind me, just over my shoulder, breathing right down my neck, but it's like it can't find me, like it won't find me if I don't move, but as soon as I move, as soon as I breathe, it's going to know I'm there and it's going to get me.'

Walter opened his eyes. Dr Feldman was right there, in his chair, right where he had been when Walter last looked.

'That's it,' he said. 'That's all.'

8.
ANOTHER DAY IN PARADISE

Another day in paradise, Walter thought cynically as he closed the front door behind him. It was Tuesday morning and he was on his way to the train station, en route to another day at the office.

He stopped for a second, his hand on the door handle, and surveyed his neat-as-a-pin front yard, his driveway, the nature strip, the road and the various other houses he could see along the street. There were no storm clouds this morning, no sun-shower, and everything looked ordinary and a bit drab, the colours duller than they had been the other morning. Walter remembered the feeling he'd had then that something was wrong—aesthetically unconvincing he had called it—but now, suddenly, with his hand on the door handle, his mouth a little open, he saw it differently, and he wondered whether he had it the wrong way around. Perhaps it wasn't the sun-shower that was unconvincing, nor the shiny-bright, not-quite-there-yet Wintergardens. Perhaps it was him. Was that why it didn't feel real? Because he didn't belong in it?

He stepped gingerly off the porch and walked down his front path. He picked up the plastic wrapped newspaper which had been thrown on the lawn. He felt for just a couple of seconds, for as long as it took him to walk from the front door to the footpath, disconnected from what he was doing. He felt as if he was wading through someone else's world, picking up someone else's newspaper, on the way to the train station to catch someone else's train to someone else's job. He didn't think in those exact words, of course, the words didn't exist, but he was aware, blankly, of the feeling of them, a gnawing in his gut like he was hungry, a gap somewhere in his head, a blackness as if there was something he didn't know yet, or some potential he hadn't quite achieved. Something. Something else.

He shook his head a little and continued on towards the train station, with his briefcase in his left hand and the still-wrapped newspaper under his arm, taking however many steps it was towards the Wintergardens train station. The same amount of steps he'd taken every other morning he walked to the train station. He would count them one day, those steps. It might be interesting to know if the amount of steps varied or remained exactly the same.

He gave a little nose-breathe of laughter.

The day he did that, he would know he was mad.

*

That morning was Walter's regularly scheduled monthly appointment with Dr Feldman. His appointment, as usual, was for 8.30am. Dr Feldman, though, was already behind schedule—how this was possible so early in the morning Walter didn't know, but he took a seat and resigned himself to wait.

The waiting room was furnished with cheap chairs, erect and uncomfortable, and tattered magazines, mostly trashy women's magazines, but a few selected for male patients—there was a *GQ*, incredibly old and without its cover, multiple copies of *Men's Sport and Fitness* magazines, and a copy of *Punch*—surely that hadn't actually been published for years now? Walter picked up the newest looking magazine—the less hands that had pawed at it, he felt, the better—and sat down to wait for his appointment. He didn't read the magazine though, flipped it open on his lap and didn't even look at it. He was watching the clock. It was 8.44am, and as he watched, the second hand of the clock ticked through the seconds, *tick tick tick*, and it became 8.45am precisely.

Nothing happened. Again.

Of course nothing happened.

Walter sat perfectly still, his legs crossed, the magazine open on his lap. The Receptionist sat behind her desk, tapping away in a desultory manner at her keyboard. There was a siren, somewhere far away, out in the streets, but otherwise nothing, and the seconds continued to tick by.

Walter flinched as the water cooler belched up a random water bubble. He felt the beating of his own pulse through his neck in his wrists and ears.

The phone rang and again Walter flinched.

The Receptionist answered it.

'Good morning, Dr Feldman's office.'

He looked back at the clock. Ten seconds to go. On the home straight now. Five, four, three, two, one. And it was 8.46am.

He relaxed his shoulders.

*

After the accident and his subsequent stint in hospital, Walter had been through trauma counselling which had been handled by a specialist firm, The Australian Centre for Post Traumatic Mental Health. Most often they dealt with people traumatised by having a workmate die unexpectedly, often on construction sites, where deaths were, if not common, then at least frequent relative to other workplaces.

Walter, of course, knew the odds of dying in various workplace accidents. He knew the most dangerous workplaces. He knew the most dangerous rooms in the house, from the kitchen which was the most dangerous, perhaps unsurprisingly, to such weird rooms as the sewing room where, to his knowledge, no-one had died in the last year. He knew the dangers of driving, the most dangerous ages, the most dangerous roads and the critical speeds. He knew where to be sitting in a car, bus, plane or any other sort of transport to maximise the statistical chance of survival in the event of a crash. In a train the safest place was generally the middle carriages—the front carriage was dangerous if the train crashed into something, the rear carriage dangerous if you were rammed by another train. The middle carriages were safest, officially, unless, that is, a random accident happened, something like a road overpass collapsing on the middle section of a train—well, there were no odds, as such, for that.

He'd never been to a psychiatrist, psychologist or psychotherapist before, and on his first visit he had found himself wildly reassured by the appearance of Dr Feldman, who looked almost exactly as Walter had thought he should. He was a bearded, rumpled looking man somewhere in his fifties, bear-like and lumbering, who wore small glasses perched halfway down his big nose, over which he peered with bright eyes and a no-nonsense manner. There was a vague smell about him of cigarettes and peppermint.

Dr Feldman had an office in a small block in Brunswick amongst other doctors, dentists and architects. The block had been built in the late seventies and was one of those sturdy, thick-set buildings featuring tumbled, beige brick and thick untreated wooden beams around the eaves and across the ceilings of the offices. The windows were floor to ceiling and made of yellow smoked-glass which gave a twilight, firestorm kind of glow to the outside world. It was, Walter thought, the perfect place for Dr Feldman with his daggy-bummed corduroy trousers, his smoky smell, his beard, his profession.

Walter was, he admitted to himself, a little disappointed that on his first visit he wasn't asked to lie down on a couch. Instead he and the doctor simply sat in chairs across from each other and chatted. No couch, no notebook, none of that. They didn't talk about the accident, not at all that first visit, but about Walter and his work and his life.

Walter was not a vain man. He was very well aware that people weren't all that interested in him. So at first it had been odd to tell a man things about himself that no-one but he knew, that no-one else was in the least interested in knowing. Once or twice in those early sessions Walter felt acutely aware that everything he said was as dull as dishwater, but he went on, got used to it and then, eventually, found he was enjoying it. Dr Feldman was paid to listen to him and that made it easier to talk—he was released from the social expectations of conversation, the need to listen, the need to respond. The rules and regulations of conversation, the awkwardness he found in interaction of any kind in the world outside, didn't count with Dr Feldman. This was all about him, Walter, and it had never, ever, in his entire life, been all about him.

Dr Feldman got up from his desk and took off his glasses as Walter entered.

'The dreams have started again,' Walter blurted out straight away.

'U-huh,' the doctor said, as if completely disinterested. He reached out to shake Walter's hand, then indicated a chair near the smoked-glass window, popped his glasses back on his nose and flipped open a folder on his desk.

'About the accident?' he asked, although it was more a statement than a question. Walter nodded his head, then realising the doctor wasn't looking at him said: 'Yes.'

'U-huh,' he said, tapping the files with a pen. 'The same as before?'

'Yes,' Walter nodded. 'They're … well, they're pretty much the same as before.'

'Do you want to go through it again?' Dr Feldman sounded bored at the prospect.

Walter shook his head, and felt it in the ropey muscles at the back of his neck. He relaxed his shoulders.

'Shake it out,' Dr Feldman said, looking up.

What?

The doctor made an odd movement with his shoulders, as if doing a shoulder-only Mexican wave, then he revolved his head around on his neck and shook his hands out.

'Do it,' he said.

Walter did the thing with his shoulder and neck and then shook his hands out just as the doctor had. He then sat with his hands politely on his lap, waiting for the doctor to continue. Dr Feldman was still over at the desk at this stage, but now he slapped the topmost folder closed, threw the pen down on his desk and came over to sit across from Walter.

'Are you dreaming through to the end yet?'

'The end?'

'Do you get out? Do you get to the bit where you see daylight and get out and survive?'

Walter took a deep breath.

'No,' he said rather darkly. 'I don't. It ends before I can get out. I wake up before I get out.'

There was a pause as Dr Feldman regarded him over the top of his glasses.

'But you did get out, didn't you? In real life I mean.'

'Yes. Oh yes of course. I know that. We've been into that quite a bit, in the past, haven't we?'

'U-huh,' the doctor agreed. Then: 'Do you have any idea why the dreams might have started up again?'

Walter nodded.

'People keep … they keep reminding me.'

'Who's reminding you?'

'A man, a reporter. Raking it all up again. He said … he wanted to interview me … and then.' Walter paused.

Should he? He may as well.

'The other day, there was a man … on the platform.'

'The platform? What platform?'

'The train platform. On the way to work. I was standing there. He was next to me.'

'And?'

'Well, he spoke to me. It was a bit unexpected. You know, you don't usually, well, I don't usually talk to people at the train station.'

'What did he say to you?'

'He told me not to get on the train.'

Walter paused there, watched the doctor carefully for a reaction, but there was no visible one.

'He told you not to get on the train?' Dr Feldman repeated. 'Are you sure?'

'Yes, of course I'm sure.'

'What did he actually say?'

'He said just that: *Don't get on the next train.*'

'Really? He turned to you, directly to you, and said that? Out of the blue?'

'Yes.'

'How odd.'

'I know!'

'There was no other conversation before or after?'

'Well, yes, a little. About the weather. The train being late. Nothing really. Just chitchat. Meaningless chitchat. Then that about not getting on the train.'

'Why did he say it do you think?'

'I don't know. There wasn't time to talk to him. He got on the train.'

'And you didn't?'

'No. No I didn't. I couldn't. It sort of threw me a bit, you know? It was so unexpected. And then of course the whole train thing, it's not very far beneath the surface I suppose. I felt agitated. I felt like I couldn't get on the train.'

'Quite understandable in the circumstances.'

Walter sighed, smiled slightly.

Yes, he thought—understandable. Quite understandable. He felt encouraged to go that step further.

'There is one other thing,' he said. 'It's a stupid thing really. But did you see in the papers? The stabbing on the train?'

'Yes, I saw that.'

'That was the train.'

'What train?'

'The train that morning. The one I didn't get on.'

Dr Feldman nodded slowly with his lips pursed, looking at Walter. After a while he spoke again.

'What do you think would have happened if you had got on the train?' he asked.

'Well … who can say? How can we know?'

Dr Feldman nodded again.

'I do know the odds though,' Walter continued. 'The odds of dying from assault with a sharp weapon. It's one in one thousand eight hundred and ninety three.'

'Quite long odds really.'

'Yes, that's what I thought. But there's the other side of the coin isn't there?' Walter grinned, as if savouring a punch-line to come. 'The one! It's got to be somebody!'

'True. True. But Walter, you survived. You weren't the one. Not on the train last week, and not one year ago. You survived that crash.'

He knew that. They'd been into it again and again. He had survived. He was a survivor, the only survivor on a train carriage that had been crushed like a tin can by a collapsed overpass.

*

At the end of the session Dr Feldman suggested that perhaps he should start seeing Walter more regularly, just until things quieted down on the dream front. They made arrangements for Walter to come weekly for a length of six weeks, after that to be re-assessed. Then the doctor showed him out into the waiting room and left him with his Receptionist to find an appointment time.

'What about next Monday at 8.45am?' she asked.

Walter stared at her for a second or two.

'You're joking?' he said.

'No,' she looked at him. 'Why?'

Walter gave a subdued laugh and said: 'Can we make it 9.00?'

9.
EIGHT FORTY-FIVE

That evening when Walter got home his car was sitting in the driveway, back from the repair shop. He went in, greeted Maggie, then got the key to the car and came back outside. Maggie followed him, a half-finished cigarette in her fingers. Walter pressed the key and the central locking *bip-bipped*. He opened the driver's side door, examined the new glass in the window, then got in the car and sat there for a moment or two, sniffing delicately.

'It's gone, Walter,' Maggie said from outside the car. She opened the passenger side door and sat in the car, her arm extended to hold the cigarette outside. She watched Walter continue sniffing the air.

'I can't smell anything,' she said. 'It's gone.'

OK, perhaps she was right. He couldn't smell anything, either, except the cloying smell of some sort of fabric deodorant, but he wasn't convinced. What would it be like when the deodoriser smell was gone? He would reserve his judgement. It seemed alright, certainly, but it was more than just the smell, it was the fact he was sitting there with the knowledge that someone had broken into this car, stolen his wallet and CD player and left behind a displeasing odour. He felt it. He couldn't help feeling it. Sure, it would probably go away, that feeling, he'd probably get used to it, but for now, it was there. If Maggie didn't get that, then Maggie was …

'You saw Dr Feldman today?' Maggie asked, interrupting his thoughts.

He looked at her.

'Yes,' he said.

'You told him the dreams have started up again?' Her voice was blunt without being entirely uncaring. When he nodded, she turned her head towards the open passenger side door and took a drag on her cigarette.

'Not in the car, Maggie,' Walter said. 'Not now that it's been decontaminated.'

Maggie rolled her eyes.

'Come on,' he shooed her towards the door. 'Out. Out.'

She blew smoke deliberately all over the car interior then got out, slammed the door and stalked back up to the house.

Walter made a clicking noise with his tongue and flapped his hand to wave the smoke away. He too then got out of the car and went inside.

Maggie really was too provoking sometimes.

*

Walter found himself in his study again at 8.45pm that night and again he was watching the clock. He smiled for a moment at how ironic it was that watching the clock had taken on a whole new meaning for him. Then the smile faded. He didn't like that he was doing this, didn't like it at all, but all the same he couldn't tear his eyes away from the clock as it ticked past 8.45pm and all the way through the minute until it was officially 8.46pm. When this had happened, he exhaled and went out without looking at the clock again.

*

The same thing happened at work the next morning. There was an 8.30am staff meeting. Dev was chairing the meeting and each of the teams that reported to him had a rep there to report on what had been going on in their areas over the last month. It was Walter's turn to represent his team. They were not the most useful meetings, Walter thought—everyone listened to things they didn't really need to know and in the most part weren't that interested in, waiting until it was their turn to talk about what their team was doing, knowing full well that no-one else in the room really needed to know or was really interested. Then one lucky person, again randomly chosen each meeting and that morning, Walter sighed with relief, not him, would type up minutes and circulate them to all staff members in all of the teams. No-one read the minutes, he suspected, which was never really necessary as there were never any 'actions' out of these meetings, being as they were, for the purpose of 'information sharing'. In other words, Walter thought, the whole thing was a complete waste of time, except for the fact Dev was able to report up that he had 'facilitated communication'. On the plus side there was the catering which was usually rather good and that morning consisted of some pastries with icing sugar on them, juicy berry muffins and percolated coffee.

At 8.44am Walter was in the middle of one of the pastries, nodding at a colleague who was going on about something—he wasn't sure quite what because he wasn't listening, was instead surreptitiously watching the clock. When it ticked over to 8.45am the droning voices of the others faded and all he could hear was the ticking of the clock as the minute ticked through. At 8.46am it was as if he faded back in, tuned in once more to the conversation going on around him, except—he sat up a little straighter—there wasn't any conversation going on around him, and everyone seemed to be staring directly at him.

'Decided to join us again Walter?' Dev said.

Oh crap.

'Sorry.' Walter madly shuffled his papers on the desk. 'Sorry. Sorry. Is it me?'

'When you're ready,' Dev smiled condescendingly.

*

After the meeting, a meeting Walter didn't think it was exaggerating to call *an absolute fucking disaster*, he went directly to the men's toilet to blow off a bit of pent up steam.

'Crap!' he said bursting in. 'Shit shit … bloody … shit.'

He couldn't believe that he had made such a fool of himself in the meeting. How embarrassing just zoning out like that, staring at the clock like a complete nutjob. A slack-jawed tool. How could he have called attention to himself like that? Made such a fool of himself?

He walked backwards and forward a few times in front of the basins, looking at his reflection in the mirror. He even went so far as to hit the bench with his open palm, but that only stung him and didn't quite work—he wasn't the type that could make those sorts of angry physical gestures without looking a bit foolish.

He could never have imagined in a million years a moment when the *time*, his old friend the time, the rigid, tick-tock-ing, inevitable time, would turn on him like this. It felt like a personal affront, like they'd purposefully poisoned one of the few constants in his world.

His thoughts hit a speed-bump right there.

He stopped moving and stared at himself in the mirror.

They?

Did he just say 'they'?

They who?

Calm down, he thought. Calm down.

'Imagine your anger,' he began, but got no further.

What was that smell?

He sniffed at his hands. They didn't smell of anything particularly, maybe the icing sugar from the pastry. He turned on one of the taps and washed them, washed them quite vigorously, with three squirts of hand-wash. There was a lot of lather. He rinsed, dried his hands and sniffed them. Could he still smell it? He sniffed again, then sniffed his wrist. Was it his wrist? The cuff of his jacket? But he hadn't even been wearing this jacket when he sat in his car that day. His wardrobe at home must be contaminated.

'Bloody … shit,' he said, throwing the paper towel towards the bin—another violent gesture that he wasn't able to pull off, as it missed the bin, scudded off across the floor and came to rest near the cubicles.

That's when he noticed feet under one of the cubicle doors.

Oh no, he thought. *What have I said? Was any of it out loud? They heard me! Whoever it is, they heard me.*

He headed for the door and blundered out of the men's toilet.

*

Walter had found himself getting less and less sleep over the next few nights. When he did manage to sleep he more often than not had the nightmare and woke up, but he was also finding it increasingly difficult to get to sleep in the first place. The moment he lay down he had a million things churning through his head—stupid, useless, little things about work, or long-standing niggles about Maggie, worries about the car, or of course the warnings, thoughts on what they meant and who might be behind them. Sometimes he felt he had an answer, but in the morning when he tried to remember what it was, he either couldn't remember what the profound revelation had been, or did remember but found it utterly meaningless.

He got up the next morning late and thick-headed with a cumulative lack of proper sleep. He showered and dressed, skipped breakfast except for a coffee, walked to the train station and caught quite a late train for him, the 8.05am express. He unwrapped his newspaper and glanced in a desultory manner through the headline stories without really taking any of it in.

Later, just outside the North Melbourne train station there was an announcement by the driver—they were being held up by a defective train and there would be a short delay while they waited for a platform to free up. The train sat for some time in the middle of the rail yards just outside North Melbourne. At first, as was usual with these sorts of delays, the passengers remained in their own world, but as the delay grew longer the feeling in the carriage changed slightly—people began fidgeting, began looking out the windows, trying to see the station and see if anything was happening, they popped their ipod ear-buds out of their ears and looked at the time. Some people even made eye contact with others and exchanged comments on the unreliability of the train system. When the delay stretched on further some made phone calls to workmates or whoever they were going to meet in the city, saying that they were stuck on a train and were going to be late. For so many people five minutes made all the difference.

Walter was aware of the slight increase in activity in the carriage as the wait stretched on. He felt it himself, a buzz of agitation. He had felt like this before when trains had been delayed. He always felt slightly unnerved being in a stationary train in the middle of nowhere, or at least not at a platform. It was perhaps the fact he couldn't communicate with the driver, or that there was rarely any real idea of how long the delay was going to be and so it felt, maybe, as if it could be open-ended. Perhaps it was that he was, in effect, trapped, that he couldn't open the doors, except by using the emergency handle. On these occasions the carriage felt, to him certainly, but perhaps to others also, a bit more closed in, a bit airless.

Walter was aware that there was something more behind his own agitation that day. He had caught the train at 8.05am. He knew from the time it took to make the journey to the city, and from a guess that they had been delayed already about five or so minutes, that it must be fairly close to 8.45am. *The time*, his old friend and, he thought with exaggerated bitterness, his newly minted enemy.

He was on the verge of checking his wristwatch, the very edge of slipping his suit coat and shirt sleeve back, when he felt a spurt of resolve. He was not going to check the time. It was ridiculous. Why should he? Why should he care? Why on earth should he be agitated about it being 8.45am and he in a stationary train outside North Melbourne station? What was there to be agitated about? In fact, in his head he decided that he *downright refused* to be agitated about the fact the time might be 8.45am.

Damn that man in the lift and his warning—*beware eight forty-five*. Ever since then he had been acutely aware of that exact time, both am and pm, had counted it down as if observing a minute of silence. He was annoyed with himself and embarrassed. It was as if he was betraying himself, as if some soft, naïve, gullible part of him was undermining what his sane, sensible conscious self knew—that there was no such thing as precognition, that the 'warnings' he had received, both of them, could not possibly be real or true or accurate in any way. Yet every morning, every evening, at 8.45 there was the minute of silence. He felt like some primitive, intuitive instinct was wriggling its shoulders within him wanting to get out, and he didn't like it.

So he refused, he just plain refused to look at his watch. He told himself he just had to stop himself, not think about it. Like any bad habit, the best way to stop, in his opinion, was cold turkey. He was in charge here. His rational, regular, everyday, tick-tock head was in charge and it said that there was no reason to worry about the time, or know the time, or think about the time.

At that moment he was acutely aware of his wristwatch on his wrist. Normally he never felt it, of course, no-one ever did once they were used to wearing a watch. But then, right then, he was aware of the weight of it, the grip of the band around his wrist, the way the back of the watch, smooth as it was, had been warmed by his skin. It felt heavy and hot.

He wasn't going to look at it. He shook his head. It was a silent stand-off between he and his previously unacknowledged superstitious self, and he was going to win.

At that moment the train began shunting forward again. The relief in the carriage was palpable. The driver came over the PA system with a word or two announcing that they were on the way again and apologising for the delay.

At North Melbourne station the train pulled up to the platform, the doors opened and people got off and then on. All the while Walter studiously avoided looking at the clock on the station platform. He also found that his right hand was closed over his left cuff, effectively gripping his wristwatch. When he noticed this he took his hand away and put it in his lap, relaxing both of his arms.

When the train arrived at Flagstaff Station he got off with a great gob of people, moved towards the escalators and rode up towards street level where he and his fellow passengers surged out of the station and onto the street.

As he strode out from amongst the milling pedestrians, he felt a sense of relief and pride. It must surely be past 8.45 now! Surely. He had done it! He had resisted looking at his wristwatch, resisted the desire to know the time. But even that thought, that brief wash of relief and pride was a betrayal—the time didn't matter, *what mattered was not caring what time it was.*

He looked over his shoulder to see if there was any oncoming traffic, whether he could dart across the road. At this exact moment his mobile phone rang. He fumbled it out of his coat pocket and flipped it open to answer it. As he did so he noticed the time—it was precisely 8.45am.

He stopped dead in his tracks so abruptly that another pedestrian just behind him, disoriented by Walter's sudden dead stop, swerved to avoid walking into him, knocked his arm, stepped awkwardly on the edge of the gutter and onto the road. Before Walter could properly take in what was happening, a bus streamed past his face. He felt it roar directly past him, right past his nose, and a strong buffet of wind pushed him back on his heels. At the same time there was the sound of the hydraulic brakes of the bus, and the sound of the bus hitting something, something not metal, something that made a dull thud.

Walter stepped backwards once, then once again, further away from the gutter. He could see the bus not far away. It had stopped, but he didn't see anything in front of it, or under it. He saw people rush from all around and crowd around at the front of the bus. Some kneeled down. Others stood back, some with their hands at their faces. He heard the sound of voices raised. Some of them sounded more authoritative than others. Soon he heard sirens approaching. He didn't see anything of that other pedestrian who had stepped past him, knocked past him and stepped onto the road right in front of that bus. He didn't see anything of whatever it was that had happened to that man. He didn't want to.

All the while there was only one thought in the back of his mind, the thought that it could have been him.

A mobile phone began ringing. It was the same ring tone as his own phone. He patted his coat pocket, but then he remembered. Of course, it wasn't there. He had dropped it. That man had knocked it out of his hand. It must be on the ground, on the road, near the body or under the bus. The phone stopped ringing.

Walter went forward and made himself known to the emergency workers who had arrived. He told one of them that he had been very near, in fact right next to the man, when he had stepped off the gutter onto the road.

'Is there anything you … want from me?' he asked.

The paramedic said he didn't think they would need anything, but took Walter's name and contact number just in case.

Walter didn't quite feel comfortable asking his next question, but what else could he do? He told the officer that the man under the bus had knocked his, Walter's, arm just before stepping onto the road, and as a result he'd dropped his phone, on the road, right, well pretty much right where the body was.

'I wonder …' he said, wishing now that he'd never said anything about it—he felt heartless and stupid and conspicuous. 'If you find it. Perhaps you could ... It's a Nokia,' he finished lamely.

The paramedic looked at him with distaste.

'I'll let you know,' he said darkly.

*

Walter didn't go to work that day. He took a sickie. He was at a bit of a loss at first as to how to call in sick without a mobile phone. What, he wondered, not very originally, did we do in the days before mobile phones? There were no public phones anywhere in that corner of the city. Probably there were, but he couldn't remember where and couldn't see any. In the end he just turned around, went right back into Flagstaff station and went home.

Maggie was surprised to see him, but was on her way out. She was off to the boutique, she said, had other appointments and shopping to do later in the day, and in the evening was out with her girlfriends. He didn't tell her about the accident. He merely said he wasn't feeling well and would spend the day in bed. She nodded and left. When she had gone Walter called Dev and left a message on his voicemail—thank God he didn't answer—saying that he had witnessed an accident, had been severely shaken by it, and wouldn't be coming to work.

By the time he had done all this Walter was feeling legitimately ill. He had a horrible headache and all he wanted was sleep. He took a couple of pain-relief tablets and a couple of sleeping tablets. He put on his pyjamas, closed the curtains and climbed into bed. He left his socks on, which was more comforting, and pulled the doona up to his chin. The room wasn't dark—it was not sunny outside but there was a very white-bright cloudy sky, and the curtains didn't fit properly, so the light seeped around the edges. It wasn't in the least conducive to falling asleep, but with the help of the pills, Walter's head, pounding on the pillow, soon stopped pounding so hard and started to become mercifully foggy.

One thing occurred to him just before he fell asleep—he wouldn't have to worry about observing a minute's silence at 8.45 any longer. That, at least, was something of a relief.

*

Walter didn't normally have people clamouring to contact him. He never got emails, except for work ones, which he answered promptly, with a 'cheers, Walter Kovak' automatic signature at the end in an italicised font, which seemed incongruous underneath his generally more officious writing style. He didn't get many calls on his mobile. The calls he did get were mostly from Maggie—it seemed there was always something she needed, or had forgotten to pick up. Sometimes people from work would call—occasionally Dev would leave a message, some note or instruction about work for the next day that he had forgotten to impart during the working day.

'You were out of here so fast,' he might say. 'I didn't catch you to tell you about ...' whatever it was. Walter suspected that these calls were less about passing on information than just making sure that he, Walter, knew that it had been noticed that he was out of there at 5.00pm on the dot and that this perceived clock-watching wasn't appreciated. But Dev could *go get fucked,* Walter thought. His hours were done at 5.00pm, so he was quite free to leave. Equity Insurance wasn't a charity and he wasn't working there for fun. Walter refused, point blank, to return any calls from Dev, ever.

He thought grimly that his mobile phone was really only a way for others to check up on him, or instruct him, so that he never, really, escaped the people who wanted to check up on him or instruct him. For this reason Walter hadn't thought it important to bother about getting a replacement mobile phone when his had been lost at the site of accident that morning, and of course by the time he had a headache he wasn't thinking about anything much. Even if he'd been in the pink of health, it wouldn't have occurred to him to rush around getting a new phone, a new SIM card, it wouldn't have occurred to him to try and arrange to access his mobile phone voicemail to see if he had any messages, to see if anyone had been trying to contact him that day, as he lay dead to the world in that not-quite-dark bedroom.

When he finally woke up, groggy headed but not headachy any longer, he found that it was dark and quite late. Maggie, as she had told him that morning, was presumably still out with her girlfriends. He must have slept the day away.

He padded into the kitchen on sock-clad feet to get a drink of juice and noticed the answering machine light was blinking. He saw on closer inspection that there were seven messages. Odd, he thought. More than usual. Someone must have been trying to contact Maggie quite urgently.

But seven messages? That was a lot.

That's when he remembered the call that had come in at precisely 8.45am that morning, just before the accident. Who had that been from? He tried to remember if he'd seen the caller id, or whether he'd simply seen the time before the phone was jolted out of his hand. He hadn't been aware of seeing any caller id, but the more he thought about it, the more he felt he actually had seen something, and that he knew exactly who had been calling him. This, along with the seven messages, was ominous.

Walter pressed play on the answer machine.

'You have seven messages,' the electronic voice said. 'First message.'

'Walter.' It was the blokey, slightly dismissive voice of Steve Groves, a broker with a firm connected to Equity Insurance. After his accident Walter had entrusted Steve with investing his insurance payout, a rather substantial lump sum. In spite of Steve's best efforts, Walter had insisted on investing it in long-term, safe (boring, Steve had said) investments rather than risky ones, and the money generally just sat around accumulating interest at snail's pace. So Walter rarely heard from Steve.

'Just called your mobile,' Steve's voice continued. 'But it went to voicemail. I really need to talk to you, mate. A-sap. Give us a call in the office.' Yes, he really said 'a-sap'.

Walter's heart sank. He might not be a superstitious person, but he knew, he just *knew*, with incredible, frigid certainty that everything was not as it was meant to be with his investments. He knew because he saw, for just a second, as if out of the corner of his eye, or in a mirror reflecting something behind him—he saw that there was something else going on here. When he tried to focus, though, he saw nothing.

Twice now, he thought. *Twice.*

10.
MAGGIE KOVAK GOES ON THE RECORD

Michael Everaardt was sitting outside a café in St George's Road in Fitzroy North. It was a small place in a run-down Victorian terrace building, with a warren of small rooms running back from the street, furnished with Formica tables and old kitchen chairs.

Maggie had suggested they meet there, it being just down the road from where she worked. Michael had walked past the boutique on the way. It had a single dress in the window on an old dressmaker's dummy and nothing else. It was the sort of place he had never been into and, he thought, this was unlikely to change in the immediate future.

He had spent the two days between the phone call and their *assignation*, as he put it to himself, thinking about what he might ask her, about how he would behave, what he would say. It was important, he thought, to get her on side in the first few minutes and keep her on side throughout the whole conversation. He was, he felt confident of the fact, able to converse easily with all sorts of people, and he felt up to the task of putting Maggie at ease. He was also, he knew, good at flirting in a non-confrontational kind of way that women usually responded to. He would see whether that was appropriate in this case and if so, would go for it. At least he'd got to first base—well, a kind of first base—and had got her to agree to a meeting. He hadn't thought he'd get even that far to be quite honest. It must all have been in the timing. He wondered about that again and again—the whole why now, why him stuff—but he no longer pondered it deeply. Nor was he suspicious because it wasn't in his nature. Generally, he felt confident about the meeting. How hard, he asked himself, could it be?

When she finally showed up, about two minutes later, Maggie trumped all his carefully thought-through plans about how he would act and what he would say. Any thoughts he had about being able to shape the course of the conversation disappeared. She was, he knew as soon as he saw her, not the type to be managed. He saw her after she had already spotted him. He looked around to his left (he had expected her to be coming from the right—the direction the boutique was) and there she was, walking directly towards him (he remembered that walk, remembered it from outside the hospital) smiling politely, and in the last couple of steps she extended her hand. Michael stood up and extended his hand also.

'Michael, is it?' she asked unnecessarily, taking his hand.

'Mrs Kovak,' Michael said. 'Thank you for agreeing to see me.'

She didn't respond to that, other than with a tight smile.

She turned her head and gestured to the café.

'Shall we go inside and find a quiet table?'

They chose a table in the back corner which had an L shaped banquette of hard, cracked leatherette. They were slightly removed from other tables and there was a sense of privacy.

'Thank you for seeing me,' Michael said when they were seated.

'You already said that.'

'Ha,' he laughed a short staccato bark of laughter. 'Well yes, I did, didn't I?' OK, so he was nervous.

Maggie didn't respond, but she did give him a small smile, as if to put him at ease. Michael smiled back and examined her face openly. He found her quite attractive. She wasn't beautiful as such, in fact her features were quite ordinary, but it was the colouring and the quality of the various elements of her face that he found attractive. Her skin for example was evenly toned and while it was lined slightly around her eyes it looked like it would be incredibly smooth to touch. Her hair was a dark shade of brunette, he noticed, now that he was seeing her close-up, not black as it had seemed to him at a slight distance at the hospital, or in photographs in the newspaper. Her lips were quite thin, but nicely shaped, her teeth regular and even, and her eyes dark blue, with no flecks or flaws.

He was reminded of the description of a woman in a story he'd once read—*she was beautiful, but she left it alone.* He had never thought much about it before, but found now that he liked the idea.

'So what would you like to know?' she asked.

That disconcerted him. He hadn't planned on jumping straight into the conversation that way. Usually reluctant interviewees wanted to know the ropes, they wanted assurances and disclaimers and a fair idea of what the end result would be before they'd begin talking. Some also asked if there was any money in it. But she didn't, after all, appear to be a reluctant interviewee. Even so, he began tentatively.

'Well, it being the first anniversary of the accident, I've been asked to write an article on the survivors, how they've got on since the accident, how their lives have changed.'

'How the women who were pregnant at the time are coping with motherhood? That sort of thing?'

Michael didn't quite like her tone there—dismissive of exactly the sort of thing they were wanting him to write.

'That sort of thing, yes.'

'And you want to interview me? Profile me?'

'Yes, certainly.'

'And my husband?'

'Him too if you think he'd be interested.'

'He wouldn't.'

She said it simply and firmly.

'OK.' Michael shrugged.

'So. Without him?'

'Without him?'

'Are you interested in me?' She asked. 'Without him?'

He found himself disconcerted by her. Not by her direct, blunt conversational style—although, yes sure, that was disconcerting also—but by the way she looked at him. It was too steady, too intrusive. Mere strangers meeting for a coffee like this, they didn't maintain that sort of eye contact, they let their eyes wander, perhaps over the menu, if there was one, or over the people passing by in the street, but she wasn't doing this, she was looking directly at his lips when he spoke. (He wondered, for a silly second, whether she was lip reading, but of course she had no need to. That's what it looked like though.) And then, every now and then her eyes dropped to his throat, as if she looked at, what, the dip in his collarbone just above his t-shirt? Very definitely heading south of the border.

He was used to such direct appraisal from sexually interested women, but this didn't appear to be like that, even alongside what had been, surely, quite a loaded question. *Was he interested in her without her husband?*

No, he decided, she was direct without being at all coquettish or suggestive. She merely had, he supposed, an unconventional gaze.

Once again he wondered how old she was. It was what he'd wondered when he first saw her at the hospital that time. He guessed she was in her mid 40s, possibly even edging up to 50. Her husband, he knew from pictures, looked slightly younger than her. He wondered whether he could ask her age.

'You're wondering how old I am?' she asked.

'Yes. How did you …'

'Men do,' she said. Then after a pause. 'Young men.'

'And?'

She ignored him. 'Are you going to answer my question?'

'Yes,' he said. 'I'm interested in what you have to tell me just as much as anything your husband might have to say.'

Maggie smiled at him, as if acknowledging the way he framed his answer. Nodded.

'Never say never, hey?'

'You mean?'

'You won't get him. He won't speak to you. And even if he did, it wouldn't be any good.'

'No? Why not?'

Maggie watched him for a moment before she said carefully in her phone-answering Mrs Robinson voice, 'Because he doesn't remember a single thing about the accident.'

Michael blinked at her a couple of times. Her face was unreadable.

'He doesn't remember?'

'A single thing.'

The twitch of a smile started on Michael's lips.

'No shit?'

'Post-traumatic retrograde amnesia,' Maggie said.

Michael's smile broadened. This was his scoop? The sole-survivor, last-man-standing, luckiest-man-alive, great-white-hope for an eye-witness interview to top all eye-witness interviews, the elusive Walter Kovak *didn't remember a fucking thing*. It was priceless.

He burst out laughing, a good big, hearty laugh, with the full-tilt pantomime of thigh-slapping and rocking back and forward on his seat. It was a gutsy laugh, no half-measures about it, and when he was finished, he found Maggie watching him with frank appraisal and a little crook at one corner of her mouth.

'That was obviously worth it.'

She had no idea!

*

Doctor Feldman had told Walter way back in their first session together that he had been diagnosed with: '... what we call post-traumatic retrograde amnesia.'

'OK,' Walter had replied noncommittally. 'So what do other people call it?' Back then, in the early days, he behaved like a recalcitrant teen in his sessions with the doctor.

'It's not uncommon after accidents. A number of people who were on the same train as you have been diagnosed with it. Most, for example, remember being on the train, remember coming through the last station, but many of them don't remember the actual impact.'

'U-huh.'

'Most of the time it's only a few seconds that are lost, usually right before and covering the actual moments of trauma. Sometimes it's longer, a few minutes, sometimes much longer, days, months, even years.'

'That's what they told me, yes.' Snippy.

'I see here in your file that you appear to have lost a week, maybe two weeks prior to the accident. They're a bit hazy on exact times.'

'It seems that way, yes.'

The doctor closed the folder. Put it aside. There was a pause before he spoke again.

'You don't give a shit do you?'

Walter snapped to attention.

'About … what?'

'About the amnesia.'

'Give a shit? I don't know about … giving a shit. I suppose I do.'

'You suppose you do?'

He shrugged. Teen again.

'You don't want to remember?' the doctor asked.

'Do I have to?'

'Well, no, you don't have to, I suppose, if you don't want to. I understand that. It is important though, that you acknowledge what happened to you.'

'Acknowledge what happened?'

'You got out.'

'Oh right. Yes, I know. I got out. I do *acknowledge* that.'

The doctor frowned at him, then softened, as if forgiving him for his bad behaviour.

'Don't worry about it,' he said kindly, more kindly perhaps than Walter deserved. 'Don't force it. If it comes back, great. If it doesn't, it doesn't matter.'

After a moment Walter softened also.

'So it really doesn't matter?'

'Matter?'

'I can be … healthy without remembering?'

'Of course.'

'Even with this black spot in my head?'

'Even with the black spot.'

*

'So where do you want to start?' Maggie asked Michael Everaardt after he had calmed down and stopped laughing.

'We can start wherever you like. The day of the accident. Where were you that day yourself?' The laugh had obliterated Michael's nerves. He felt relaxed.

'I was out,' she said simply. 'I got a call when I got home. It was the hospital. They told me that he, that Walter had been in an accident and that I should come. They said they expected he would be fine, but that I should be there. Very ordinary really. I mean it's horrible when it happens to you, but you also realise later that those calls, being called to the hospital like that, it must happen all the time, to other people, you know? Daily.' She stopped for a second, considered, then went on. 'Anyway, I went in. I didn't realise at the time that it had been this huge accident on the train. I hadn't heard about that. It may have been on the news, perhaps, but I wasn't watching the news. I didn't have the radio on. So I didn't hear anything about it. I thought possibly he'd been in a car accident. I mean, when you hear someone's been in an accident and is in hospital, you just presume a car accident. They happen so often, don't they?'

'They didn't mention what had happened to him over the phone.'

'No. No they didn't. I don't think they do if they can help it.'

'And at the hospital?'

'Well, when I arrived, this was late in the afternoon, about 4 o'clock, I suppose, I went straight up to Walter and saw him. He was groggy, but awake. I suppose they had given him something. Perhaps painkillers. They didn't tell me exactly what they'd done to him, but I understood there was no need for any sort of surgery at all. He was cut and scratched and beginning to bruise, but there were, they said, no internal injuries. He had, though, had a quite severe knock on the head. They wanted him to stay there, in the hospital, for a day or two. For observation, they said.'

She stopped for a second and looked at Michael. A shade of amusement and something else, guilt maybe, came over her face.

'It was actually quite funny seeing him there. I know that's probably not the right thing to say, but too bad. I remember noticing how rigidly he was tucked into the bed. The blanket and sheet were folded down and smooth over his chest. He was straight up and down like a ruler with feet sticking up at the end. His hands were tucked in alongside him. The first thing I thought was that he would just love those hospital corners. He's always been a very tidy man.' She said it ruefully as if it were a great virtue that she did not value overmuch.

'I must admit, I never really felt there was any danger. I mean, he was cut about a bit, but the doctors, they said he was physically fine. It was just the head injury, they said. They would need to do tests when he was stable, to make sure there had been no damage done.'

Michael nodded and smiled. He was surprised that Maggie talked so smoothly and easily about that time, especially given that she had refused to do so up until this moment, almost a year after the event.

'And when did you find out what exactly had happened to him?'

'Well, more or less immediately of course, although it took a while, I admit, for me to realise the … scope of it. They had told me at the hospital that he'd been in a train accident, but they didn't tell me the details. Again, I thought it must have been some accident with the car—possibly at a level crossing or something. You just don't think these things, these terrible, horrible big disasters, happen to people close to you. But when I left the hospital, I noticed other injured people. I hadn't noticed them coming in, but when I left it occurred to me that Emergency was kind of clogged with people and extremely busy. Then there were reporters. They came up to me as I was leaving and asked if I was Mrs Kovak. I didn't answer them. I didn't, at first, understand why they would even be asking. I just naturally shied away. Later I knew what they wanted and avoided them on purpose, but at first it was just a natural instinct for me not to speak to them.

'When I went home that first night to pack a few things and head back into town, I saw pictures of the accident on the news and in the papers. I saw the extent of it, how horrible it was, and seeing this I began to get scared for Walter. Before, well, it had seemed that it was OK, because he only had cuts and bruises, and that he would be fine, but seeing those huge big chunks of road and concrete all piled up like that, and thinking about the fact that he'd been hit on the head, I got more worried about what they would find when they did those tests.

'I also saw on the news that there had been only one survivor from the carriage that was underneath the overpass when it collapsed, and that this was Walter. There was a picture on the front of the newspaper, of a man getting to his feet in the middle of the rubble, the dust cloud all around him. That was Walter. You couldn't really see, it was just a silhouette, but it was him.'

Michael didn't say a word about being responsible for the very photograph she referred to, but his guilt about it made his cheeks feel hot. He imagined her saying something like, 'What kind of person would take a photograph at a time like that?' But she didn't.

'Anyway, I kept coming back to the hospital. Coming back and coming back. Ignoring the journalists. There were more and more of them. They came to my home too, but I had the police around and they left me alone.

'Walter was fine. He seemed fine. He knew who I was, that I was his wife and my name was Maggie. They took him through things very slowly, you understand, gradually. He knew his name and my name and his address and who the Prime Minister was and things like that. They asked a lot of questions, sort of broader, coming back to more and more specific. When they asked him what date he thought it was, he wasn't quite sure. When he answered though, he was a month out.

'They asked him if he knew what had happened to him and he just shook his head and said he had no idea. He presumed, he said, that he'd been in some kind of accident. A car accident perhaps? The same as what I presumed, but he said he had absolutely no memory of it happening whatsoever.'

'So it's not just the accident he has no memory of?'

'We can't be exactly sure, but the doctors say weeks. One. Maybe two. It's difficult to be sure.'

'So the official diagnosis was post-traumatic amnesia?'

'Retrograde. Yes.'

'And the treatment?'

'There is no treatment. The doctors told us that long-term memories tend to return gradually, over time, not in one big bunch, but like pieces of a jigsaw puzzle. Sometimes, they said, memories wouldn't return at all.'

'And have the memories returned? Any of them?'

She paused for a second, nodded, then changed her mind and shook her head.

'Nothing significant.'

She turned her head and looked out along the length of the café and into the streets at the passers-by and the traffic.

'He dreams about it,' she said.

'The accident?'

'He dreams about being trapped in the carriage afterwards. In the dark.'

There was a pause, an uncomfortable pause.

She turned back to him.

'No, it's not a nice thought.'

'It was a remarkable escape,' Michael said.

'Remarkable,' Maggie agreed.

'There's never been any explanation for it, has there? I mean, why he survived. How.'

'You sound like him.'

'What do you mean?'

'When he came home from the hospital he went mad for researching the accident. Police reports and newspaper stories. He even arranged to see one of the structural engineers who had examined the scene of the accident. You know, that guy with the big moustache who's always offering 'expert commentary' on the news? Greek name. Can't remember it now. Anyway, Walter wanted to know how it was that he hadn't been crushed. He wanted the scientific explanation!' She smirked.

'And did he get one?'

'Well, he got an answer of sorts, but I don't think he found it very satisfactory. I mean, it was a fluke, that's all. Whatever it was, it wasn't something you could get a scientific explanation for. Some things are bigger than that, don't you think, even if you're not spiritual or religious or whatever? You just thank your lucky stars and move on, don't you? You don't get a Greek engineer to try and provide a scientific explanation.'

'What did he come up with?'

'Pretty much what I just said—it was a fluke, but he said it with different words, like displacement and probability and so on. In the end it was a lot of not very much. But Walter wanted to know. He was after some sort of explanation.'

Michael pondered that for a second.

'I think I can understand that, wanting an explanation.'

'But you wouldn't do it would you? Go to a structural engineer to work out, mathematically or however he did it, why you survived, the odds of you surviving that particular accident?'

Michael began to shake his head, then stopped.

'I'm not sure. I might.'

'You wouldn't.'

'How do you know?'

'I just know. You wouldn't. You're sensible.'

'Walter isn't sensible?'

'Oh God yes, he's sensible.'

'Then?'

'But he's unreasonable.'

Michael nodded.

'I can understand, though, wanting to know.'

'Perhaps,' she said, easing away from the conversation slightly and looking very much like she wanted a cigarette break. 'But there isn't an explanation, is there? Displacement and probability aside. It just happened, didn't it? Some things just happen.'

If she was less of a lady, thought Michael, she would have said: 'Shit happens.'

11.
A POTATO IN THE SHAPE OF THE VIRGIN MARY

Walter was eating his lunch in the churchyard and feeling flat as a tack. It had been one of those days. Hell, it had been about seven or eight of them! He had got a bit of attitude from Dev that morning for his recent poor attendance record and his last minute call in sick the day previously, but he had managed to brush that off easily enough. His headache had gone, but he had a sleeping-pill-hangover. He felt heavy and plodding, his head dull and unresponsive, unable to do anything except stare ahead and endure dumbly. He had, however, been unable to escape that one conversation with Steve, his broker.

'Mate,' Steve had said when Walter answered his phone. Walter winced—he hated being called mate. 'I was trying to contact you yesterday.' Well yes, obviously he had been trying to contact him. Apart from the seven messages on the answering machine at home, there were four on his phone that morning at work, and who knows how many on his mobile phone—which he had heard nothing about from the police, by the way, not that he expected to, and not that he really wanted to have the phone returned.

Walter had suspected what was coming with Steve and he was right. Those 'safe' investments of his hadn't proved so safe after all. He didn't actually hear much of the explanation, he was waiting for the cut-to-the-chase bit—how much was left. Apparently Steve could have 'unloaded' the stocks right up until midday the previous day, if he had been able to reach Walter in order to get his 'sign-off'. But as it was, Steve said, there was not a lot they could do about it, as all the funds were now frozen.

And the cash, the dollars, the insurance payout Walter had got after his accident?

'How much is left?' he asked Steve.

'Well, that's the thing.'

'Half?'

'It depends you see …'

'A third?'

'… on how much we get in the dollar.'

'A quarter … less than a quarter?'

'Walter, mate, I'll let you know as soon as I do.'

Steve said goodbye, repeating that if only he'd been able to contact Walter the previous day, everything might have been averted. It was therefore, he was hammering home none too subtly, Walter's fault.

Heaven forbid, Walter thought, *I might not be contactable by phone every bloody, jiggery second of every bloody, jiggery day.*

He hung up, none too quietly, at which point Dev poked his head over the partition and raised his eyebrows in an I-heard-that-and-you-know-there's-a-no-private-phone-calls-in-the-workplace-policy kind of way, which is actually quite a simple look—disapproving. Walter raised his hands in an it-was-an-incoming-call-and-by-the-way-fuck-you kind of gesture in return.

His escape for lunch was a relief. He went to the churchyard and sat on his usual bench, unwrapped his sandwich and munched on it, mouthing at the food without interest, crumbs falling on his lapels. Little city sparrows hung around the periphery and darted in every now and then when they judged it safe.

Life, he thought, was crap. Although it could be worse—he could have gone under that bus yesterday. That could have been him. Perhaps that should have been him.

Last night, after checking those seven messages on the answering machine but before Maggie had returned home from her jaunt with her girlfriends, Walter had gone to his study, had picked up *The Odds of Dying*, and had used it to calculate the odds of being run down by a bus. The statistics in the little book weren't broken right down into every type of vehicle involved in pedestrian fatalities, didn't distinguish between buses and other vehicles, so the eventual odds he came up with were probably stacked a bit lower than they would be if it were buses only, but it was close enough—the odds of a pedestrian dying from being hit by a vehicle on Victorian roads were quite low at one in five hundred and eighty eight. He had written this information in his little pocket diary alongside the others, then looked up to see that Maggie had apparently arrived home silently and had sidled up to the doorframe and been watching him all along. The look on her face had been almost unreadable—she could have been concerned or suspicious, or conceivably both.

'What are you doing?' she asked mildly.

'Nothing.' A silly response. The little book of odds was in his hand, which he made no effort to hide. The very fact that he held it so rigidly at his side made it suspicious. Maggie had looked at the book briefly, then had turned and left without a word.

After finishing his lunch Walter was sitting on his bench, straight-backed and ergonomic, staring dismally at the sparrows, when an old woman came out of the church. He had seen her around before. He didn't know her name but called her The Italian Widow in his head—as opposed to The Young Widow, which was Missy. She was a very short, stout woman, and wore the unrelieved black of Italian widows, layer upon layer of black—dress, cardigan, stockings, walking shoes and black beads. Usually, on the days that he saw her, she would come out of the church and sometimes sit for a while in the garden and rest, having been inside doing, well, he didn't know what—churchy things. Walter had not been inside this particular church. He didn't know what it looked like in there, but he presumed dark and glowering—it was a small bluestone building with a squat little steeple and very small windows, with quite murky-looking stained glass over which there was a thick wire mesh. It was a very small church, taking up not much more than a normal everyday suburban block in Wintergardens, unimposing, hidden from view by hi-rise buildings either side.

The Italian Widow looked around the churchyard garden for a spare seat. Her head moved jerkily and she looked, Walter thought, like a cocky, black Bantam hen. After a moment she came towards him.

'I can share this seat.' It wasn't really a question.

Walter nodded and said, yes, of course she could share the bench. Then he moved across to one side. He had been perched right in the middle of the seat—of course, right square slap-bang in the middle as if he'd measured it with a ruler. Walter knew he was spatially sensitive. He had read up on the subject in a book called *Body Language and Spatial Relations.* He found it very interesting really, that sort of thing, like where people sat on public transport, which seats were filled first and which were always the last to go, where they sat on park benches—usually right in the middle if no-one else was there, but at the extreme other edge if there was someone else using it—or which urinal men used if they went into in a public toilet, furthest from the entrance and if someone else was in there, the one furthest removed from him. It was all about preserving personal space in the midst of a whole lot of other people. Walter had found it an intriguing study, and afterwards he was always, somewhere in the back of his mind, aware of his own personal space, and how other people's personal space interacted with it. Interfered with it might be a better word.

The Italian Widow sat down on the other end of the bench. She was quite short and her legs didn't reach the ground. She attempted to lodge her handbag, a big black one, and a green recyclable shopping bag on her lap, but there wasn't much lap there, due to the overhanging bosom, and so she put her bags on the seat beside her, arranged her arm securely through the straps and clasped her little fingers together in front of her, which was a stretch but which she managed. It was a bit of a production all up, and Walter watched out of the corner of his eye, vaguely interested, vaguely amused.

Once settled, The Italian Widow sat there, alert and secure, looking at the world, the churchyard, the people in it, the sparrows, the bustle on the street beyond the black iron railings of the fence.

It wasn't like Walter to ask questions of strangers, not at all, but he was sufficiently groggy-headed this morning with his sleeping-pill-hangover for the usual social conventions hard-wired into him not to matter. Plus the woman, this Italian Widow, reminded him, in a way, of his grandmother, fussy and plump and alert and essentially European.

'What were you doing in there?' he asked.

Her head turned towards him only slightly, as if she had a very stiff neck, or an invisible neck brace on, but her eyes snapped all the way round. She looked at him for a moment then faced front again.

'Praying.' She shrugged her shoulders. 'What else?'

Walter nodded. Of course praying. He was always asking questions that other people thought were stupid. What he meant, though, was, 'Why?'

After a moment The Italian Widow continued.

'I light a candle for my grandson,' she said. 'Tony. Antony. Like his grandfather. He goes to Bahrain today for work. His flight is at three fifteen. I light a candle for him, for a safe journey and to be happy and healthy. Also, I light a candle for my dead husband, Antony, and for my daughter and her no-good husband, because their son is going away and they have not been getting on so well lately.' She rocked a little in her seat, re-settling her hands together. 'It's easier than going to see them, you understand.'

Walter smiled.

'I'm sorry to hear about your husband.'

'Thank you,' she said. 'But I can't pretend it wasn't a relief.'

'He'd been failing, had he, towards the end?'

The Italian Widow shook her head.

'Fit as an ox,' she said.

Walter nodded.

She again turned her head slightly towards him, her sharp eyes swivelled again.

'You know,' she said. 'I found a potato once in the shape of the Virgin Mary.'

Walter wasn't sure he'd heard right. First they were talking about her dead husband, then they were talking about a potato in the shape of …

'In the shape of the Virgin Mary, yes.' The Italian Widow turned back to look over the church yard. 'There was even a little root that looked like a halo.'

A potato in the shape of the Virgin Mary?

'I was just a girl, in a village in Calabria. I looked like a young Sophia Loren back then. We all did actually. Very common, that look, very common. Anyhow, I was peeling potatoes one night, helping Mama prepare dinner, when I saw it, The Virgin Mary with the little baby Jesus. Right there in the sink.

'We kept it, the potato. Didn't eat it. Uncle Angelo put it in the bread bin. The neighbours came in to look. Then it was in the newspapers and other people came to look, from further away. To look and pray. And of course to see me. To kiss my cheek. Shake my hand. Just to touch me. Some of them even asked me to bless them.' She laughed a little and rocked on the seat. 'It was crazy. Special and wonderful. But crazy. I remember it all my life. That time. That potato.'

Walter sat still for a moment. He didn't quite know how to react to this story about a potato in the shape of the Virgin Mary. The Italian Widow noticed his inactivity and, after another sharp look at him, nodded as if he had spoken.

'So you see, I know what it's like.'

What it's like?

'To be touched by the hand of God.'

Walter stared at her but did not speak. Why was she saying this, talking in that way, as if she knew something, understood something of him, as if she was sympathising with him?

'I know how you must feel,' she said.

'Me?'

'Mm-hm.'

'You mean …'

'Amazed. Confused. Wondering all the time: 'Why me?''

Wasn't that how he felt? Hadn't he and Dr Feldman talked about that very thing time after time in their sessions?

Finally he spoke.

'You know … about the accident?'

She shook her head.

'I don't know anything about any accident.'

In a second Walter had adjusted his ideas. If not the accident …

'Then …'

'You've been visited?'

Visited?

'Haven't you?'

He nodded. Immediately he nodded. He didn't believe what he was hearing, didn't believe what this woman was saying to him, didn't really understand what 'visited' meant, and yet he nodded, without thinking about it. What was wrong with him, nodding in agreement with this ridiculous woman?

But she was right.

'Who are they?' he asked.

'Do you believe in guardian angels?'

It was like a slap across the face to Walter. *Guardian angels?* Here at least was a question he knew the answer to.

'No! No, I don't believe in guardian angels.'

'You sound quite positive.'

'I am.'

'Well you should believe. They're here. Amongst us.' She paused for a second. '*Do not neglect to show hospitality to strangers, for thereby some have entertained angels unawares.* Hebrews 13:2.'

'But why do they …' he didn't finish his question.

'They're sent to earth to do God's bidding.'

'I don't believe in …' but he couldn't finish that sentence, not sitting right there in a churchyard next to an Italian widow whose only non-black piece of jewellery was a silver cross. He couldn't say out loud that he didn't believe in God. But he thought it, guiltily, and slapped it back almost immediately.

'I'm sorry, but I'm not religious.'

She pulled her mouth down at the corners in a grimace and shrugged immensely. It was a familiar European gesture, one his grandmother had often used. He knew that shrug.

Walter looked at her with a sense of amusement and even fondness. He found, quite unexpectedly, quite suddenly, that he believed her.

No, that wasn't quite right—he didn't believe her, he didn't believe in angels as she believed in them, but he suddenly understood something of that belief, understood the shape of it, the heft and breadth of it, understood a little of it without feeling it himself. Like a museum piece behind glass, he could see it, he could walk around it, he could put his nose right up against the glass and peer at the surface of it, study it with his mathematical mind—but he was still removed from it, and after a moment or two he became aware of his own reflection in the glass of that display case, he met his own eyes and felt his usual perspective return.

Having understood The Italian Widow, if only for a second, he felt OK about asking a question within the context of the woman's own beliefs.

'You're not … one of them are you?'

'One of what?'

'A guardian angel?'

Unexpectedly the widow tittered with laughter.

'Oh heavens,' she said. 'The idea.'

Walter blushed and after a moment got up and walked away.

*

Not being the sort of man to disobey pedestrian crossing lights— especially not since the accident— on his way back to work Walter pulled up abruptly when the red man started flashing, and remained safely on the curb.

You're not one of them are you?

Why on earth had he blurted out such a silly thing?

He knew, of course, exactly why—because he expected another random warning from another random person, someone on the train or in the lift or on the street.

Walter turned his head. There was a middle-aged man, dressed in a suit and a tie, someone he didn't know, right beside him, also waiting to cross the road. The man turned to him and smiled briefly. Walter turned back and looked straight ahead.

Please, he thought. *Don't say something to me about the weather.*

The little green man started flashing and Walter took off across the road, ducking and weaving through the oncoming pedestrians. He looked back when he reached the other side and saw that he'd left the man for dead. He smiled. *Gotcha that time.*

He hurried the rest of the way back to the office at a brisk walking pace, breaking every now and then into a lumbering half-jog for a few steps. It was the gait of a man in a dreadful hurry, but a man who didn't want to commit to actually running.

There were two more pedestrian crossings between him and the office and at each one he was convinced there was someone watching him, not the same man all the time, someone different, some new corporate so-and-so looking at him, just to the side of him where he couldn't see them.

He kept his eyes front and centre, blinkered, and when the lights changed he shambled off in his brisk-walk-lumbering-jog, before anyone had a chance to say anything to him.

He reached the Equity Insurance building, ran up the steps, past Mick and David who were having a sneaky fag break, into the lobby where he pressed the lift-call button.

It occurred to him that if there actually had been people looking at him out there it was no doubt more to do with his shambling run through the streets than anything else. The guys from work, Mick and David, out there on the steps, they probably thought he was a weirdo for scurrying past them like that, but he didn't care.

He didn't care.

Of course he did, but …

*

'You think a lot about the opinion of others, don't you?' Dr Feldman had asked him out of the blue.

'Do I?'

'Well, don't you?'

'You said it.'

Dr Feldman was silent.

'Maybe I do,' Walter admitted after a while.

'Does it matter? Other people's opinions?'

'Well … yes, yes I think it does. Of course it matters. I mean, there are rules aren't there?'

'Rules?'

'Things you do, things you don't do. Society's rules. I don't know. Rules of engagement. We all play by the rules, don't we?'

'Some people don't.'

'Yes, but they're sociopaths.'

'And what happens if you don't play by the rules?'

'I don't know. Nothing really. I mean, not the unspoken rules. Non-legal rules. Nothing happens. Except … I suppose people look at you sideways, don't they? If you don't fit in. They think you're a freak.'

'A freak?'

'Well, not a freak. That's a bit harsh, maybe. But … I don't know … I suppose they just notice you.'

'And the object is not to be noticed?'

'I don't know … the object of what? You're putting words in my mouth.'

'Do you want to be noticed?'

'Not particularly.'

*

With a start Walter realised that a man was standing close by and a little behind his right shoulder, also waiting for the lift. He flinched slightly. The man saw the flinch and smiled at him, then turned back. He was a young Asian man, with spiked black hair and a sharp suit. He paid absolutely no attention to Walter. At least, Walter thought, that's what it looked like.

A lift arrived and the doors opened smoothly—it was empty. The young man stepped in, pressed the number for his floor and stood back. Walter stepped towards the lift, hesitated for a moment, then resolutely stepped back. He was not getting in a lift with only one other person. OK, so he didn't believe in God and he didn't believe in guardian angels, but there was no need to tempt fate was there? The last time he had been in a lift with only one other person …

The young man looked at him as the lift doors began to close. He reached out a hand, presumably to the door-open button, but he was not in time and the lift doors came together and didn't open again.

Gotcha. Walter smiled again.

He knew, though, that he couldn't win at this little game of his, not forever. He was, after all, surrounded by strangers, every day, on the streets, in the lifts, in the train, millions of them. They were everywhere, these anonymous corporate strangers with green apples for heads—chances are one of them would get him eventually.

*

'Thank you for that, Mrs Kovak,' Michael said. 'I really appreciate the time you've taken to speak with me.' He smiled at her and she returned the smile, a little more warmly at this end of the interview, but that wasn't unusual in Michael's experience.

'I hope it's been of some use,' she said. She began fussing around collecting her purse and her bag and her scarf.

'Oh I think it has.' He paused. 'Although there is one thing I'd like to clarify,' he said.

'Yes,' she said.

'The car.'

'What car?'

'Walter's car.'

She stopped fussing about with her belongings and looked at him.

'What about it?'

'You say that when you found out your husband was in the hospital you thought he'd been in a car accident.'

'Yes, that's right.'

'So I presume that when you arrived home his car wasn't there.'

She paused for a moment.

'No,' she said eventually. 'No, that's right. It wasn't.'

'Which means that Walter was out in the car that day.'

'Yes. Yes, he had been.'

'And yet he was on the train from the city to Wintergardens when the accident happened.'

Maggie considered him, looked at him again in his too-personal zone, as if summing him up one last time.

'They found his car three days after the accident,' she said.

'They?'

'The police.'

'Where?'

'In the city. In a multi-level car park. Presumably it had been in there ever since the day of the accident.'

'Was there something wrong with it?'

'It started OK when the police let me bring it home.'

Michael's attention wandered for a second as he followed his own train of thought.

'So why did he drive into town but take the train home?'

She shrugged.

'He doesn't remember. He doesn't remember the day of the accident, the week of the accident. He doesn't remember why he drove into town and he doesn't remember why he didn't drive home.'

'It doesn't make sense,' Michael said.

Maggie watched him for a moment.

'I know,' she said.

12.
AT THE PINK FLAMINGO MOTOR-INN

It happened in the lift on the way back up to the office. Walter had waited until a group of people came into the lift lobby, but it still happened, even in a crowded lift. He was standing, with his nose right at the door when someone from very close behind him spoke. It was a woman's voice this time, which was something different. She didn't mention the weather, or anything about stopping all stations, she just launched straight into it without any conventional conversational preamble. *Go home immediately*, she said.

Walter spun around and looked at the woman behind him, but apart from being a woman, she was, in every other regard, just the same as the other two—generic in her corporate uniform, a navy suit jacket and skirt with some logo embroidered on the breast pocket, with a forgettable face and conservative up-do.

Everyone in the lift looked directly at him as if outraged and a little unnerved by his about-face. Surely, their collective expression said, it wasn't the correct etiquette to stand facing inwards like this, staring at them all. Was this man mad?

Walter opened his mouth to speak, but closed it again. He didn't ask the woman to repeat what she'd said, or what she meant, or why she'd said it, or anything like that. She would, he knew, be just like the other two. She would look at him suspiciously, and not admit what she'd just said. He turned back to face the doors of the lift, shoulders slumped, looking like a man who's just been paint-balled in a corporate team-building exercise.

The woman got out one floor below his.

Go home immediately, she had said.

He looked at his watch. It was only 1.56pm. How was he going to get this one past Dev after all the time off he'd had the last week, a sick day and time off for his appointment with Dr Feldman?

More importantly, what was waiting for him at home? Remembering the outcome of the first two warnings, he wasn't sure he wanted to know.

Although it didn't quite fit, did it, this warning? The stabbing on the train, the accident in the street—the first two warnings had apparently been about avoiding those incidents. This one seemed different somehow.

Maggie, presumably, was at home.

Was she OK?

When he got back to his desk he rang the home number but there was no answer. He tried Maggie's mobile, but she didn't pick up. There was nothing for it—he would have to go home.

He couldn't not go. Could he?

*

When he arrived home he hung up his coat in the hall, put his briefcase down in the hallway and called Maggie's name. There was no answer. Not home? Given the latest warning he felt inclined to check the bedroom, check all the rooms of the house, make sure it was empty. He loosened his tie, paused, sniffed at the air, then moved through the entry hall, sniffing again carefully.

Surely it wasn't the smell from the car? Surely the same rank-smelling man hadn't broken in here at home?

No. No, it wasn't the same.

A couple of steps further and the smell was strong enough for him to recognise it. Gas.

He rushed into the kitchen. The smell there was almost overwhelmingly sickly and strong. He went to the stovetop and found one of the burners turned full on but unlit, the unseen gas hissing out of it. He turned it off and the hissing stopped, but the smell remained, thick in his nose. He coughed, covered his mouth with a tea-towel and opened the window over the kitchen sink. He waved the tea-towel around in the air as if this would help disperse the gas, but eventually he realised it wasn't doing anything and stopped.

It was then that he heard a sound from the front door. Maggie! He got there in time to see her come in. She had her handbag open and hooked on her wrist and was searching through it for her cigarette lighter. She had an unlit cigarette between her lips.

'Where have you been?' Walter asked sharply.

'Walter!' Maggie jumped and the cigarette fell from her lip to the floor. 'You scared the shit out of me.'

Walter picked the cigarette up off the floor.

'No smoking,' he said, wagging the cigarette at her like a finger. 'Not in this house. Not today!'

'What are you on about now?' Maggie put her bag down on the hall table.

'You left the gas on!'

She moved past Walter to the kitchen where she went to the stovetop, checked all the gas taps and opened another window. Walter followed her.

'So where were you?' he asked.

Maggie stopped moving around. She stood still, with her back to him. There was a pause—a long, edgy, slightly ominous pause. Walter didn't immediately notice the quality of that pause.

'Shopping,' she said.

'No bags,' Walter said.

'I didn't see anything I liked.'

If he had been able to read his wife better, he might not have said what he did next.

'Who were you with?'

'No-one.' There was a dangerous edge in her tone, unmistakable now, even to Walter. Challenging, threatening. He immediately drew back.

'Oh, right,' he said. 'Of course. Sure sure.'

Maggie finally turned away from the sink to face him.

'Who do you think I was with?' she asked with a dangerous smoothness.

'No-one. No-one. I just wondered if ...'

'What?'

'Nothing,' Walter said. 'No. Nothing.'

'You think I'm lying?'

'No ... no ...'

'What do you think I've really been doing?'

Maggie moved closer to him. She eyed him steadily.

'Tell me. Tell me what you think I've been doing, Walter? You and your dirty little mind?'

Oh crap.

Walter knew where this was going. He'd flicked Maggie on the raw, said the wrong thing, and when she got her back up she would fight. But he didn't have to fight back. He said nothing and his expression shut down. There was another frigid little pause as Maggie took in his expression.

'No?' She turned away to the bench again. 'I didn't think so.'

She moved away, went back to the front door, picked up her bag.

'I'm going out for a while. When I get back, I don't want you to be here.'

What? Again?

'For how long this time?'

The only answer was the front door slamming.

*

The Pink Flamingo Motor-Inn was halfway between Wintergardens and the city along a main arterial road. There was a central square of concrete with parking spaces and painted-on numbers, and built around that were twenty-four rooms over two levels, with a balcony running all the way around the second story.

Constructed of grey breeze-blocks painted a very faded pink colour, it was the kind of place that still advertised 'colour TV' as an attraction, although this may merely have been a very old sign as it was as faded as the 'flamingo pink' exterior.

The rooms were small boxes with en-suite sized bathrooms and plywood doors. There were mini soaps individually wrapped on the basin, and a roll of toilet paper on the toilet roll holder, but not much else in the way of amenities other than the bed, the lamp, the radio in the headboard and the colour TV, which was, perhaps surprisingly given the rest of the room, not an old analogue set but a huge flat-screen digital.

One way or another Walter had spent quite a few nights there at the Pink Flamingo Motor-Inn. When things came to a head as he put it to himself, or indeed to Dr Feldman when they had discussed his recurring homelessness, when there had been a disagreement, this is where he came. Not that their disagreements were ever all that acrimonious. Maggie was moody, sometimes mysteriously moody, Walter felt, but while she could be antagonistic, she was rarely argumentative. She seemed to be spoiling for a fight and shying away from one at the same time. Walter knew he could be niggardly and pedantic, but he disliked any sort of direct conflict and just as he had done earlier in the day, he actively withdrew from any sort of fight or argument. So while their altercations were relatively regular, they were also stunted little spats, after which one or the other of them would immediately vacate the premises in order to 'clear their head' and come back with a new perspective, or to be more accurate, come back without a new perspective but never say another word about whatever had been the problem in the first place. It was a tactic that had grown out of their tendency to miscommunication, and apart from the fact that it obviously didn't work, Walter thought he and Maggie had a good system going. They certainly didn't 'fight' as such.

Sometimes after one of their disagreements Maggie would take off and spend a night in the city, go to a show or a movie, then stay somewhere in town for the night, or with one of her girlfriends, or Arlette. She transformed trouble on the home front into a night on the town and seemed to actively enjoy herself, returning home exhausted but refreshed, as if from a long-weekend holiday.

When Walter felt the need to get out, or was asked to as it usually happened, he came to the Pink Flamingo Motor-Inn. He enjoyed his breaks as much as Maggie did, enjoyed the feeling of being in exile that came with staying at a two-bit, duct-taped, shabby old motel. It was as if he had been granted pardon from the buttoned-up routine of his everyday life, as if he had a permission slip to walk around in his singlet and boxers, drink beers and watch footy. He did none of those things of course—he was not really a sports fan, wore his usual polo shirt tucked into his trousers, and while he did have a drink in his hand, and it was, officially, hard liquor, it was a gin and tonic mix in a can, the second of two he had purchased on the way, and two was his limit.

He put the can on the bedside table, sat on the bed, bounced a couple of times experimentally, then lay back and put the Achilles heel of one foot between the big toe and the second toe of the other foot. He stared at the ceiling. It was one of those made of pre-fabricated panels that were all-over-prickles with little whipped up peaks of what—plaster, plastic?

'What do you think I've been doing, Walter?' Maggie had asked. It kept going through his head as he lay there. 'You and your dirty little mind?'

It wasn't him that had the dirty mind, though. It was her. She was, after all, the one who had been unfaithful. He didn't mind, any longer, saying the words in his head—unfaithful, infidelity, affair. The whole thing for him was over and done with—the whole incident and how he had felt about it was now vague and dull as if covered with a dust sheet.

It had become slightly fuggy in the un-air-conditioned room, and his head was groggy after the two cans of gin and tonic mix. His mind wandered. He thought, vaguely, of The Italian Widow who believed in guardian angels, who, she said, came to earth to do God's bidding.

What was that line she had quoted from the Bible—something about not neglecting to show hospitality to strangers, because you may be entertaining angels unawares?

It sounded improper somehow.

What was God's bidding he wondered?

Was it always the same?

He reached over to the drawer beside the bed and pulled it out, but it was empty. No bibles in motel rooms and no couch at the psychiatrist—what was the world coming to?

If he was at home he could have done a search on the internet for information on angels. But what would it tell him? What would it change? He didn't believe in angels and he didn't believe in God or his bidding.

Who were these people, then, these complete strangers giving him these warnings? He had at one point thought those guys from work, Mick and David, could be behind it, but he didn't think that any longer. He thought back to their blank, doughy faces when he had seen them on the steps of Equity the previous day having their smoke break. They were neither smart enough nor subtle enough for this. They would do something obvious and with an immediate payoff. This was slick and obscure, so slick and so obscure that he had trouble understanding what it was all about. That was the thing he couldn't get past. Why would anyone bother? Why him? No-one bothered with him.

There was more to it, though, wasn't there, more than the warnings? There was what was happening after the warnings. Three times now. Wasn't there beginning to be a bit of a pattern?

At that point a train rumbled past—the Wintergardens line ran quite close behind the motel. Without realising he was asleep, or very close to it, Walter rocketed up in bed wide awake.

He got up and walked from the bathroom to the doorway and back again a couple of times, pacing until he felt stifled by the confines of the small room. Then he went to his suitcase, opened it and took out *The Odds of Dying*. The odds of dying an accidental death in general were low, just one in sixty nine, but the odds of dying specifically as a result of a domestic gas explosion were much higher at one in eighty-three thousand, nine hundred and thirty—higher than the odds of dying of a lightning strike he noticed wryly. He was writing the figure in his pocket diary next to the others when he was interrupted by a knock at the door. He gave a guilty start and put the book and the pocket diary back in his suitcase.

'Who is it?'

'Room Service.'

He opened the door and was instantly very gracious and smiling. Everything, he seemed to be trying to communicate, was quite alright with him—nothing to see here. A pimply adolescent boy came into the room and set a covered plate down on the little side table next to the TV. Walter had ordered a toasted sandwich from a very simple and frugal room service menu.

'Thank you,' Walter said.

The boy went to the door. Walter followed.

'So, that's it is it?' he said in the doorway.

'Sorry?' the boy asked.

'Nothing else?' Walter asked, sounding facetious.

'No. That's all.'

'Nothing else to get off your chest?'

'No.' The kid looked at him as if he was a nutjob.

'Oh. OK. No, quite right. Of course. Thank you. That's all.'

Walter closed the door slowly, aware of a sense of disappointment.

Whoever they were and whoever was behind it, he didn't know, didn't understand why they would bother with him or how it worked, or what God's bidding even was. He knew, though, that *within the context of the fiction*—he kept saying this to himself, saying it over and over again, as if it made everything OK, put everything in its place, like a lawyer saying 'without prejudice' and then being free to say anything—*within the context of the fiction* he was certain that he would get another warning from another stranger sometime soon. It had been a woman last time so it could obviously be anybody, even room service.

*

Walter had forgotten to bring his pyjamas with him and so he slept that night in a white t-shirt and his underpants, something he rarely did and which made him feel sort of reckless. It was more than the lack of pyjamas, of course, it was the whole thing—a drive-in motel, cans of gin and tonic before bed, the change in routine, the escape from Wintergardens. It all conspired to make him feel off-course and, there it was, reckless.

He slept badly and, unusually for him, he kicked at the sheets until they became untucked and the bedding slipped, crumpled, to one side. It was very un-Walter.

13.
WALTER AND MISSY CONTEMPLATE ANGELS

Saturday dawned bright and clear at the Pink Flamingo Motor-Inn. Walter sat up bleary-eyed, wondering what time it was and if his breakfast was yet in the breakfast hatch. He had never got over his childhood excitement at the thought of breakfast being delivered via that hatch. The steps coming to a stop outside the door, the sound of the hatch being opened outside, the rattle of the dishes on the tray as it was deposited, a sound that was at once in the room but not, and all the time he was right there on the other side, so close but totally unseen, which in itself was exciting to a little kid. His parents would be totally uninterested, laying-in, or showering, or smoking, or getting dressed or whatever they were doing, while he sat, quiet and still and excited and waiting for whoever-it-was to close the other side of the hatch so he could open it from the inside to reveal, *ta-da*, their breakfast. Slices of toast, not very hot it was true, in their own little wax-paper sleeves, mini boxes of cereal, a little white jug of milk, sachets of coffee and sugar, mini peel-top portions of Vegemite and honey and jam. To a child in the early seventies it had been the very zenith of excitement.

He breakfasted and thought about what he was going to do for the rest of the day. It was unusual for him to have a Saturday all to himself. His weekends were usually quite full. Much of his time was taken up at the house, with the garden, the lawn, or a number of small chores, pottering around, fixing things, tidying up. There was also, usually, something that Maggie had organised for them to do, one of the neighbour's homes they had to go to for one of those incessant BBQs, or, more depressing, Arlette's place. Or they might go out just themselves, the two of them. They considered themselves interested in the arts and would usually go and see any travelling exhibition on at the National Gallery of Victoria—they'd enjoyed the Impressionists but been less impressed with Dali. But these outings happened less and less regularly.

Walter did get a little time of his own on the weekends, and it was these stolen moments that he enjoyed the most. Time alone in the car, for example. He would sometimes extend drive-time to or from some errand, weaving around the suburban streets with one of his chill-out CDs on, looking at people's gardens, at new houses being built, taking in a different suburbia to his own.

He also got to enjoy time alone when Maggie was out by herself. These times, when Walter was alone in the house on the weekend, were like a special childhood treat, not a million miles away from the breakfast hatch, with the same feeling of urgency about enjoying it to the full, not wasting a drop. Not that he disliked having his wife around. Well, actually, perhaps he had grown to dislike it. No, that was unfair; *sometimes* he disliked it, when she was in a mood, or antagonistic, but mostly he just found that he felt slightly stifled when she was with him, like he was behaving in a certain way for her, doing what she suggested, letting the tone be set by her, as if his life was one big, 'Yes, dear'. And so, on the flipside, when she was gone and the tone was set by him, he felt released.

On these occasions, when Maggie first stepped out the door, or backed out of the driveway, his future moments of solitude, whatever they might hold, however long they were going to last, stretched out before him, infinite with promise. He would be eager and excited, hungry to get on with things. Not that he ever did anything all that special. He might simply use the time to read without being interrupted, or research something he was interested in on the internet, order books or CDs from the many and varied sites he regularly checked, looking for first editions of favourite old books, spy books from the 50s and 60s, or new books from favourite authors, new recordings of his favourite pieces of music or from his favourite chill-out artists. Or he might play CDs in the house rather than in the car, and turn them up loud, as he could rarely do when Maggie was home as it disturbed her (or else she was on the phone to a friend or had the television on and was watching some program). He would perhaps drag one of the couches right between the speakers and lay back in it and close his eyes and listen to the music, or perhaps he would stand there, in front of the speakers, swaying. Not dancing, just swaying. Or he might go to the opposite extreme, with complete silence through the entire house, which was rare when Maggie was there. She didn't like silence, she said, preferred some 'background noise'—not his music, she qualified, that wasn't background noise—so enjoying the silence was one of his favourite things to do when Maggie was out. He would let it envelope him until he realised it wasn't quiet at all. He would hear the smaller sounds that he never heard normally, the hum of the fridge, the sound of rain or wind if the weather was acting up, the sound of birds or dogs, although there seemed to be more dogs than birds in Wintergardens for some reason, the distant hum of cars on the freeway beyond the quiet of Wintergardens' walls. He felt the distance and depth of Melbourne at these times, and he liked that. Or he might wander through the house and just think about things—not necessarily things in the real world, problems at work, or difficulties he might be having with Maggie, not real things like that, abstract things. Nothing as concrete as a fantasy or an imagined life, but ways, perhaps, in which his life might be different—like what it would be like if he had a different job. Not that he specified the details. It was just a better job with a better office, a secretary maybe, and nicer colleagues who were more deferential. Or he might think of the children that could one day be in what were now merely spare rooms. He didn't imagine Maggie pregnant, or the birth, or babies—he skipped over that and imagined a little boy and a little girl, already young children, tidy and well-behaved. He imagined what sort of father he might be, kind and well-loved, but slightly strict with them when they misbehaved. He imagined these children vaguely, in an old-fashioned way, as one who knew nothing of children might, and shied away from the image quickly, sensing how unrealistic it was.

In the end his enjoyment wasn't really about any of the things that he imagined or did, but the fact that he was doing them alone. The simplest things seemed different when he was looking at them, sitting in them, living them alone. He always found that he knew how he felt, what he thought about something, only when he had a moment or two alone to sit with it, work it out. Something inside of him seemed to seep out when he was alone, expand like a hot-air balloon right there in his lounge room, nosing out corners, knocking things off the shelves until the room was full of it.

Moment by moment, as Maggie's return became more and more imminent, the gloss began to wear off his enjoyment, and it became difficult to sustain. By the time he heard the car in the drive or the key in the door, the balloon had deflated and was tucked back in out of sight, and in a way, just slightly, it was a relief. Maggie was back and with her would come the energy, the noise, the slight mess that accompanied her everywhere—keys thrown down just anywhere, a bag left in the hallway, the chatter of the real world outside, what she had done, what the traffic had been like, maybe, and what so-and-so had said, or what so-and-so had done. It was a return to normality, to a measured and stable, well, relatively stable world, the dimensions of which were known, the rules understood and his role defined.

What would he do if he had unlimited time without Maggie, no neighbours to visit, maybe even no job to go to? He would, he could quite easily, speak to no-one, see no-one, quite happily do so, until he became buoyant and began lifting up, his toes scrabbling to keep a hold of the earth.

Instinctively he felt that leading a life of such solitude would be dangerous, as if he would degenerate or disintegrate in some way, and so he felt content to enjoy it in short, contained, bursts. Time away from Maggie, time alone, was wonderful, but at the same time it was Maggie who kept him from floating away completely. In these moments he realised that he was, after all, grateful she was in his life.

So it was that the prospect of an entire weekend out of the house, away from Maggie, was at the same time thrilling and a little overwhelming. He drove to Highpoint Shopping Centre and pottered around the shops for a while, got himself a new mobile phone and SIM card, then having exhausted Highpoint he looked at his watch and found it was still only 10.45am.

He thought by default of familiar pastimes and went into the city to visit the National Gallery of Victoria. There was a travelling exhibition on that he hadn't yet seen. It was the work of a German photographer, and while he wasn't particularly interested in photography, at least it was something familiar to do.

As a distraction the exhibition didn't turn out to be at all successful. He stalked through the gallery on the balls of his feet, his hands clasped behind his back, staring at the artworks but not noticing them. His solitude that morning wasn't like other times, in that it unnerved rather than comforted him. He felt bitter that this too had been taken away from him along with everything else.

He stopped dead in his tracks. Across the room, looking at one of the photographs was Missy. She was wearing black leggings which finished just below her calves, white and tan soft-soled casual shoes, a white t-shirt with a very pale green cardigan on over it, light-weight, slightly fluffy and fitted to her curves. Her almost white-blonde hair was twisted away from her face and held by a hinged comb at the back of her head, a cocky-like crescent of hair escaped and curved out above it. There was no sign, Walter noticed, of her two daughters and yet she looked exactly what she was, a young mother.

Walter felt instantly uncomfortable and hot, as he always did when he found himself in close proximity to Missy. He supposed she had a similar effect on a lot of men. Her physical attractions were pretty obvious—the gym-toned firm buttocks and meaty calf muscles, white-blonde hair, red lips, not to mention the triple-whammy combination of tight t-shirts, big breasts and large nipples. Walter remembered the time she'd spoken to him at the barbeque and flushed crimson.

It was more, though, than just her physical attributes that made it impossible for Walter to feel comfortable in her presence. He knew that somewhere not very far below the surface his discomfort wasn't actually about Missy's overt sexuality. Sure, he wasn't the kind of man to be even slightly nonchalant alongside overt sexuality, but there was more. His greatest fear on seeing Missy like this, in a social way—a fear so vivid that it shot through him like a jolt of electricity—was that she might talk to him about her husband.

Walter decided to abandon the rest of the exhibition and make good his escape. He left the main exhibition hall in what he hoped was a covert manner, studiously avoiding looking in Missy's direction. He couldn't help it though—he turned for a look just as he slipped out the door, and as he did he saw that Missy was looking directly at him.

He walked briskly away towards the base of the escalator. He would loose himself in the permanent collection, he decided. She would never find him there. The areas of the gallery that housed the permanent collection, a warren of odd-shaped rooms that didn't seem to connect to each other in an expected way, was the perfect place to get lost in, or lose someone.

He took the escalator upstairs and walked through a few rooms and around a few corners until he felt as if he was deep within the innards of the NGV. During all this time he had passed no-one except guards who looked as if they would any second tip over in a deep sleep. He eased up a little, walked a bit slower, looked at some of the artworks he was passing. He was in a room of early European art and as he moved through it he realised that most of it seemed to be religious themed. Here were saints, here were halos. Surely, around here somewhere there would be …

It was called *The Virgin and Child with Saints*, painted in the early 1500s, and pictured angels hovering around the eponymous virgin and child.

Angels!

He looked at them long and hard. They were, he supposed, meant to be children, but they were like no children he had ever seen. They seemed smaller than children, slighter, as if they were dolls or miniatures. And their faces! What was wrong with their faces? These certainly weren't the faces of innocent children, they were instead podgy and knowing and rather sickly looking. They had wings, but they seemed to be merely sitting there, not flapping at all. They didn't appear to be hovering like hummingbirds, didn't look like they could actually do any vigorous flapping at all with those pathetic little wings. In short, they looked, Walter thought, like mangy little critters.

The room was dim and still, and even though he could hear the air-conditioning humming away somewhere it seemed slightly airless. He knew that if he thought about it too much he would begin to imagine he was having difficulty breathing, so he put it out of his mind. There was a small ottoman in front of the picture, so he sat down and thought about his own three 'angels'—very definitely in inverted commas with *finger-quotes*. He thought what he often thought, what he often said to Doctor Feldman, he thought: *Why me?*

He knew his place in the world. He didn't warrant a conspiracy of this kind, no matter what motivation might be behind it, and if it wasn't a conspiracy of some kind, if the three of them weren't co-conspirators coached into saying what they had said to him, then what? Were the warnings totally random? Coincidence? He couldn't believe in three entirely random strangers entirely randomly giving him entirely random warnings.

There was another explanation. It had occurred to him a while back, at the start of the whole thing—in fact it had been on his mind all along. *What if it was all in his head?* He was, he knew, not all there. Not mad or anything, but there was that black spot in his head. He had sustained a head injury in the accident, had lost a certain amount of time. He felt it, felt that little black spot, that shadow, almost as if it were tangible. Things, perhaps, weren't quite right in there somewhere. It wasn't a terribly happy option for him, this one, but it had to be faced. What if he was imagining it all? What if these strangers said nothing, or perhaps said entirely ordinary things and he then imagined them saying something else? What if it was all just another of the conversations he regularly had with himself?

But this explanation didn't quite convince him. Being the sort of man he was, he didn't believe his mind could play these kinds of tricks on him. He felt as if there was a higher awareness within him, a ruling body or something, and that this awareness, solid and scientific, would know if there was any monkey-business being attempted by his subconscious mind, would know it and recognise it and overrule it. He didn't believe he could fool himself into imagining those three warnings.

The only thing left, he told himself with a gesture as if squaring his shoulders, was that the people were real and the warnings were real and that it was, well, it was something totally outside his frame of reference, something totally foreign and alien to everything he had previously thought to be so.

He felt empty at the thought, lost and bewildered.

He stared at the painting.

He wondered what the Virgin thought of the angels, hovering so close and annoying with their lutes and their bugles and their leery, creepy faces. He could imagine she might at any moment swat the annoying little vermin away from her head, or kick them away from her heels, but that they would inch back slowly, hoping not to be noticed, until they were once again right there, with a proximity that made her skin crawl.

He heard a squeak, the sort of squeak that might come from a tan soft-soled casual shoe, and hard on the squeak her voice, right behind him.

'Hello, Walter.'

He jumped and hunched his shoulders.

'I'm sorry. Did I scare you?'

'No no,' he lied. He got up.

Missy looked as she always did, fresh-faced but sort of apprehensive—the look of a woman who had not had a good run with her husband, or was dealing alone with two young children and a part time job, or both.

'I thought it was you,' she said. 'I waved, but you mustn't have seen me.'

He managed not to look at her breasts, not directly, but as a result felt he was staring into her face a little too unblinkingly. He wondered if men often looked at her like this and supposed so. Either that or they ogled her shamelessly. Even so, her nipples, he noticed in his peripheral vision, the type all men have when it comes to these sorts of things, appeared not to be as on-show as they sometimes were.

Walter felt as he always did in Missy's presence, like an awkward schoolboy with his hands jammed right down into his pocket, drawing shapes on the floor with the toe of his shoe. He had, he knew, a ridiculously prudish side to him, but he just couldn't help it. Maggie had told him, many moons ago this seemed now, before they were married, that she actually found his prudishness arousing. The more he blushed or looked uncomfortable the more she wanted to say rude words, suggest rude things he could do to her, or grab his penis through his trousers. She did all of these things, all three of them at one particularly memorable work function.

'I didn't see you,' Walter lied.

'What did you think?' she asked.

'Of the photos? Oh impressive. Very impressive.'

'I liked the hi-rise,' she said.

'I'm not usually very much into photography,' Walter said.

'Me neither. I mean, I'm not much into anything really. I mean, art wise. I feel a bit of a fraud just being here,' she said, smiling at him a little. 'But you know, I just felt, oh I just felt I had to get out and do something, you know, cultural for a change, and this was the most cultured thing I could think to do.'

'The kids are in crèche?' Walter guessed.

'Yes!' she said rather wildly. 'I work on Saturday afternoons. I cheat though. I take them in first thing in the morning. This is the only time I get to myself all week—a couple of hours.'

She laughed at herself. Shrugged her shoulders.

She was, Walter realised, enjoying her time alone with the same slightly manic determination he usually did. He well understood the importance of those few stolen solitary moments and he felt, for the first time, an absence of the usual discomfort he felt in Missy's presence, a sort of kinship instead. They had something in common.

'You come here often, I suppose?' she asked artlessly.

'Well yes, I do.'

'You and Maggie are so lucky.'

Well, Walter thought dryly, that was definitely a new perspective.

He presumed she meant they were lucky because they didn't have children and could still have a social life.

'We have been trying, actually.' Walter surprised himself by admitting it. 'Or, we were.'

'Oh,' she said and turned to study the painting with sledgehammer tact.

'They don't look quite right do they?' she said after a moment, her head slightly to one side. 'The people there.' She pointed. 'As if their limbs aren't quite bending the right way.'

'No,' Walter agreed. 'Not quite convincing.'

There was a moment while they contemplated the picture.

'I saw a café just back there,' Missy said after a moment. 'Do you want to have a quick coffee with me? I've got about twenty minutes before I have to head off to work.'

'That'd be nice,' Walter said. He found that he actually meant it.

Together they walked to the small café overlooking the main hall. They ordered two coffees and took them to one of the small café tables.

'Did you consider IVF?' she asked him when they were settled.

'We went through the early stages, yes, but we put it off after the accident, until I was out of hospital and back on my feet. We just haven't … just never, quite, well, never quite got back to it.'

Missy stirred her spoon around in her latte, breaking up the chocolate heart shape in the froth that the barista had created for her, then licked her spoon with her little pink tongue.

'You don't usually mention the accident.'

Walter looked down at his own coffee. He thought of her pink tongue licking that teaspoon. He didn't like the way she looked at him. Hopefully? Or knowingly, as if she saw him differently than she did others. What was she hopeful of? What did she think she knew?

'Do you remember anything?' she asked. 'I know that Maggie said, well, told us that you had blacked it all out, the accident. Apparently that's quite common. But I wondered if, in the last year … I wondered if you remembered anything.'

'Not really,' Walter said, still looking at his coffee, stirring it and stirring it and stirring it.

'How long? How long before the accident is blacked out?'

'I don't know. A few days? A week?'

'Do you remember seeing Aristo?'

Here it was. Here was the moment he had been dreading. Missy was asking about her husband.

Aristo had died in the same accident that Walter had survived, something that Walter had been horrified to hear and also unable to process. It seemed so coincidental that a neighbour of theirs, someone he knew, was also involved, worse, had died. On thinking about it, though, he realised it wasn't necessarily all that odd. After all, it was a Wintergardens line train, and it was therefore not unexpected that there would be people from Wintergardens on the train. In fact, from every suburb up and down the line there were people who had been involved in the accident, had died, or been injured, or of course survived without so much as a scratch—a corridor of tragedy running roughly north-west from the Melbourne CBD. There had been four people in total on the train from Wintergardens proper—an older woman and her seventeen year old grand-daughter, who had been on one of the derailed carriages of the train and apart from whiplash were mostly unharmed, Missy's husband, Aristo, who had been in the carriage with Walter, the carriage that had been crushed, and had not survived, and Walter, who had.

The moment he first met up with Missy after the accident, at a dinner party at a neighbour's house, he hadn't realised she was going to be there, wasn't prepared to be faced with her, and his head spiralled and rebelled. She had taken his hand, formally, as if at a funeral or something and nodded at him. *The young widow.* Walter drew back, drew his hand back stiffly as if it was coated with something. Maggie, who had been next to him, had stepped in and murmured a few words of consolation to Missy on the death of her husband, but Walter hadn't been able to say a word. In fact, when all was said and done, he had pretty much fled. The dream feeling had come over him, the fear of something unknown, something in the blackness just behind him, and the need, the desperate need to get out, to run and flee and escape. On that occasion he had given in to it.

Maggie had come home a little later and told him it was OK. She told him that everyone understood. Walter had hated that. He didn't want people to understand. No, not that—he didn't want to be the sort of person people *needed* to be understanding about.

Nobody mentioned it again afterwards, but all the same he found himself incredibly uncomfortable in Missy's presence from that moment on. He could never walk into a room where she was, a backyard where she played with her kids, without experiencing that same feeling, the desire to run away.

This time he hadn't run. He sat there, sat across the table from her, with a coffee in front of him, and she had asked point blank if he had remembered anything about Aristo. Here he was, facing his demon and her eager, hopeful eyes.

'I don't … I'm really not sure,' he said.

She opened her purse, flipped through a couple of photographs in there, mostly of her children, but at the back was one of Aristo. She showed it to Walter and as he looked at it he could feel her watching him.

He had, of course, seen Aristo before, at barbeques and other social gatherings, before the accident, before his death, but he found as he looked at that picture that he hadn't until this moment really remembered him, not properly. It was a strong-featured face, positive, thickset, a very masculine face. He was surprised by the softness of the smile—probably the picture was taken by Missy in a romantic moment.

He wondered then, looking at the photo, at the tender smile, whether Missy had ever wished at any point over the year since the accident that instead of him, Walter, it had been her husband sitting in that unexpected air pocket, or whatever it was, when the train carriage had been crushed.

Out of the blue, looking at that photo, Walter remembered seeing Aristo on the train the day of the accident. He remembered it very clearly. There was a newspaper, he saw a newspaper, and behind the newspaper, presumably reading it, was Aristo. It was a meaningless flashback, fleeting and unwelcome as they always were, and as inconsequential as his memory of the woman doing the sudoku puzzle had been.

He blinked once, heavily, suppressing the memory of that face behind the newspaper and looked at Missy. She was looking at him with a hungry look in her eye, a look that told him he'd given himself away.

'You do remember?'

'I think so,' Walter admitted. He blushed and his eyes dropped to the tabletop. 'I think he was … reading the paper.' He squinted. 'But that's it. I mean, it's just a snippet. Very small. Very insignificant. I'm sorry.'

'Reading the paper.' She repeated it as if it was important.

Walter finished the last of his coffee and got up. How awful, he felt, that this was all he had to give her, a glimpse of her husband reading a newspaper.

She had risen also, and put her hand on his arm just above the elbow. He felt the warmth of her hand through his clothes.

'Thank you,' she said.

She did not seem at all disappointed.

*

Michael Everaardt was on the footpath out the front of a multi-storey car park in the city. He squinted and looked up at it sideways, up along its eight levels, but inspiration refused to strike.

This was the car park where Walter had left his car on the day of the accident. It was not, Michael knew, a car park he would have used in order to nip into the office, which was on the other side of the city, diagonally opposite in the CBD city grid and a good twenty minute walk away. Besides, there were plenty of other car parks much closer. No, Walter had not driven in to visit the office that day.

Michael had been over and over his notes and the reports and news items he'd sourced on the accident. There had been one mention, in a police report he'd found through a mate in the force, that Walter's car had been found here on level eight of this car park three days after the man himself had been in and survived the accident on the Wintergardens line train—but there was nothing in that report or in any other about what he had been doing in the city and why he had left his car there.

This small fact seemed odd to Michael, like a wrinkle in an otherwise smooth sequence of events. It didn't make sense, because if Walter had driven in that day, by rights he shouldn't have been on the train home to Wintergardens at all, he should have been driving. Why wasn't he? Maggie had said that there was nothing wrong with the car when the police found it and eventually allowed her to bring it home, so that wasn't the answer. Then what was?

The more he thought about it the more he found himself becoming fascinated with Walter in a new way, fascinated by the hours just before the accident, those hours that even Walter himself didn't—apparently—remember. What had he been doing? Why was he in the city? Where had he gone? And why was he on the train back to Wintergardens rather than in his car?

Michael felt he needed to know, that it was important to find out—but he didn't know why he felt this. A base journalistic or mongoose instinct? Or a childish love of the unknown—unsolved mysteries, all that stuff? Whatever it was, he had to know, but who was going to tell him? Maggie—perhaps she knew? He got the feeling that she definitely knew more than she was telling him. Walter himself? Did he know? Apparently not.

Chances were Walter had done nothing of any note that day, Michael thought. Perhaps a little shopping, or whatever it was that a man like Walter did—visited a gallery or something. He was the sort of man to visit galleries, Michael thought. Something mundane. But even the most mundane of things could seem poignant if they were shrouded in post-traumatic retrograde amnesia and immediately preceded an accident.

Michael knew better than most that the last moments of survivors, or non-survivors for that matter, prior to any horrific event, no matter how ordinary, were journalistic gold. If only he could find someone who knew.

How odd, he thought as it occurred to him, that there was no-one who could bear witness to Walter's movements that day, not even Walter himself. Michael didn't follow that line of thought anywhere, but he felt it, just for a second, he felt how unusual it was that a man could park his car in the city and do, well, whatever he did, and that not a single person knew about it. For a second Walter seemed 'creepy' to him, like a sleepwalker or a zombie or something.

He shrugged it off and again looked up squinty-eyed at the parking lot. It was a multi-level car park, with giant concrete balcony-like levels. Nothing unusual about it. His eyes counted up the levels and found the level Walter's car had been found on—the top level, level eight.

His thoughts stalled there.

Level eight?

Surely on a Sunday afternoon, an eight-level car park would not have been so full that Walter would have to go up to the top to find a vacant park.

Michael walked down a bluestone cobbled alleyway to the pedestrian entrance of the car park. He went past the auto-pay machine and found a small and not particularly pleasant smelling lift, which he took to level eight. There were no attendants, he noticed, as the whole thing was automated. No-one to see Walter's movements, or note the time he came in.

The lift opened and he stepped out onto the top level of the car park, which was open to the sky. It was mostly empty of cars, but there were a few here and there, close to the lift. The rest of the top level was a deserted expanse of concrete, parking spaces marked with faded white paint. Anonymous hi-rise buildings with darkened plate glass windows edged the car park in on both sides but the front and back were open to the streets. Michael put his hands in his pockets and strolled across the expanse of concrete, dotted here and there with little shallow puddles of water or wet spots, towards the rear wall.

When he reached the edge he put his hands on the lip of the concrete wall—it came up to just above his hip—leaned over and looked down. Quite a long way down, he thought, but not particularly high, not enough to give him a sense of vertigo.

He was looking out into Little Collins Street. Along the other side of the street there were a number of old Victorian-era buildings, oddly juxtaposed with anonymous plate glass hi-rise buildings, as they often were in Melbourne. These Victorian-era hangers-on, thanks to heritage listing, would never be knocked down, and they stood their ground down there on Little Collins Street like a row of dowdy, stumpy, immovable Victorian matrons.

Michael noticed that from where he stood he had an excellent view into the upper storey windows of one of these Victorian piles—the Albert Hotel. He knew the Albert, or at least knew of it. It had been a coffee house in the late Victorian era and was now a dingy hotel—the sort of place people stayed when they came up from the country to watch a football match—cheap but not particularly cheerful.

Where had he read something recently about the Albert Hotel?

14.
LAST VISIT TO DR FELDMAN

Walter's weekend at the Pink Flamingo Motor-Inn was over. It was Monday morning, and it dawned drab and grey, like a Monday morning should. He checked out, loaded his suitcase into the boot and drove to Brunswick for what turned out to be his last appointment with Dr Feldman.

The doctor was as rumpled and avuncular as ever. He was wearing a fleece-lined hoodie with a University logo on it that Walter didn't recognise. It should by rights, Walter thought, have been a cable-knit cardigan with a belt and a pipe in the pocket. He was rummaging through the files on his desk, so Walter took his usual seat near the smoked-glass window and waited. After a few moments the doctor found what was presumably Walter's file, gave it a slap, but didn't open it or read any of the contents, then joined him over by the window.

'How are things at home?' he asked as he took a seat.

Straight to the jugular, Walter thought. How did he do it?

'I'm not actually at home at the moment,' he admitted. 'I'm back at the Motel. It's my home away from home. It's quite nice.'

'It's not really is it?'

'Well, no, no it's not. It's awful. But it's … well, it is alright being there, away from home, just for a couple of nights. It gives me breathing space.'

'Trouble with Maggie?'

'Nothing serious,' Walter shrugged. 'Nothing new. Same old same. Trust issues. Blah blah blah.' He paused and looked at the Doctor expectantly.

'You seem keyed up today.'

Walter nodded. He was.

'What about?'

He opened his mouth to answer, took a breath, but the words didn't come out. Dr Feldman smiled.

'Spit it out,' he said.

'What? Spit what out?'

'You've got something on your mind. And no matter how awful it is, or how crazy you think it makes you look, just get it out there. There's no use making an appointment to come here and talk to me and then not talk to me. So what is it?'

Walter was rigid in his chair. OK, so this was it.

'You're right of course,' he said. 'And this is going to sound stupid to you no doubt, it sounded stupid to me, but apparently ... well, apparently I've got guardian angels.' He said it in what he hoped was a light, mocking tone, as if it was something totally silly that he was inviting the doctor to laugh about with him, but his steady, level gaze gave him away. He eyed the doctor sternly, seriously, waiting to see which way he was going to jump.

'Guardian angels?' Dr Feldman said it completely blandly. Just repeated it.

'Yes.' Walter stared at the doctor's impassive face. He waited.

'You say 'apparently',' Dr Feldman went on. 'Why 'apparently'? Is this something someone else told you?'

Walter exhaled. The world hadn't stopped turning, the doctor hadn't said: 'I'm sorry, we're going to have to leave it there as you are obviously completely mad.' As a result Walter felt he could answer this second question.

'Some Italian widow I met in the churchyard where I have lunch. She's very religious. She believes in angels.'

'I see. She believes in angels. Do you?'

'Well, no. Strictly speaking, I don't. I don't believe in angels. I don't really even believe in God. I can say that right? In here? It's confidential isn't it?'

The doctor smiled the smallest smile.

'Quite confidential,' he said. 'I'm puzzled, though. You say that you have guardian angels …'

'Apparently.'

'… apparently have guardian angels, but in the next breath you say you don't believe in them.'

'Well … in the context of the fiction,' Walter said tentatively, with the air of trying something out.

Dr Feldman didn't seem all that impressed.

'Compartmentalising,' he said. 'In the context of what fiction?'

'Well, the fiction that angels, guardian angels, exist. That fiction.'

'As opposed to the context of fact where they don't?'

'Ummm. Yes. That's right.'

'I see.'

Walter bridled a bit.

'This isn't easy for me. You have to understand. I'm in the position of having something happen to me which defies any rational explanation I can find for it. I'm left … I'm left … I don't know. I'm left in a very awkward position.'

Dr Feldman nodded.

'I can see that. Yes, I can see that. But let's go back a step. You say that you have—apparently, in whatever context you like to put them—guardian angels. I want you to tell me more about this. Are we talking about actual angels, with wings, sitting on a cloud?'

'No,' Walter scoffed. 'Not that sort of thing. This is not a religious experience, it's a … secular one.'

'But you do see them?'

'I see them, yes.'

'They appear to you?'

'I … yes, I suppose you can put it like that.'

'Then what do they appear as?'

'Just people. Ordinary people. People alongside me … Once on the train station platform. Twice in an elevator at work.'

'Is this ... are we talking about the gentleman on the train platform we spoke about last session? The one who told you not to get on the next train?'

'Yes, yes that one. There have been two others since, and they've also given me warnings.'

Dr Feldman watched him carefully for a second.

'OK, so these people who have given you warnings,' he said. 'Couldn't they be just that? People, strangers, who speak to you and give you warnings?'

'Well, yes, you're right, they seem to be just ordinary every-day people. But that doesn't make sense. Why would they do it? They'd have to be in league or something, wouldn't they? Part of some plot? And then how could they know? How could they know what was coming, what to warn me against doing?'

'Those questions you find unanswerable, but identifying them as guardian angels you accept.'

'In the context of the ...

Dr Feldman shook his head.

'In this context.' He spread his hands out.

'Then I believe ... I believe ... I don't believe guardian angels exist. But ... but I can't ignore what's happening to me. I can't ignore that. I know it's happening and if no rational explanation fits ... then there isn't a rational explanation, and I ...'

Walter paused.

'Yes?' Dr Feldman prompted.

'I have to accept ... that ... that there is no rational explanation.' Walter felt a warmth flow through him with those words, a great sense of physical release. He looked past the doctor and out the smoked-glass window to the street beyond.

'There have been three of them,' Walter said, staring blankly. 'They've each given me a warning, out of nowhere, and each warning has saved my life. First, on the train. I ... I told you about that, where the man was stabbed. I would have been on that train, in that carriage. Then, they warned me about an accident … a traffic accident … I was on my guard and I managed to avoid it. Someone else died. It could have been me quite easily. Then, the third one warned me to go home immediately. So I did. If I hadn't I'd never have got home in time to … There was a gas leak. I know they say domestic gas is safe, but … you never know. I might have been too late to …'

Walter stopped and looked back from the window. Dr Feldman nodded encouragement but said nothing to fill up the pause.

'Why me?' Walter went on eventually, a little belligerent. 'That's what I want to know. Why are they doing this to me? I don't want this. I don't want to be saved. I don't want to be special. Why don't they go and appear to someone who believes in God?'

The doctor nodded again. Walter's eyes slid back to the window.

'I'm beginning to suspect …' he slowed down a bit, breathed in and out, started again. 'They're not really there to protect me. Not really. This isn't about protection, because you see, there's always a sting in the tail. Three times now, the good stuff happens, then the crap follows. They save my life, sure, but as a result my life gets worse in some way. I'm alive, but each time it's a life a little bit less liveable. The first time, because I didn't get on the train, I took my car to work. If I hadn't done that it would never have been broken into and my wallet wouldn't have been stolen. Then my investments, my insurance payout. If it weren't for the accident on the street, my broker could have contacted me in time to avoid losing everything. Then, just yesterday, I get home in time to stop … who knows what, but get kicked out into a stupid, stupid, stupid motel. It gets worse and worse. Each time.'

He paused for a moment.

'It's like they're playing with me for some reason, stripping me bare … bit by bit. But I don't … I don't know why?'

Walter stopped talking. He blinked. He felt empty, a little sick. Dr Feldman was silent. Walter turned to look at him. His face was the usual mask, but when he spoke his voice was low and level, smooth and even, with no jagged edges. Walter noticed the difference. *This*, Walter thought, *is how he talks to the loonies.*

'Why would they do that?' the doctor asked.

'I don't know,' Walter said, turning away again, slightly dismissive now. 'I don't want to be special. I didn't want to be special back then and I don't want to be special now. I didn't ask to be the only one to survive that accident, did I? No. I didn't. I didn't want that and I don't want this. I don't want any of this. Why can't everyone just … leave me alone? Why can't they just let …'

He stalled and lapsed into silence.

'Let what?'

'Let whatever's going to happen to me happen.'

It felt good saying that, coming to that conclusion.

Dr Feldman nodded and smiled slightly.

Walter's eyes slid back to the window. He knew—looking out at the park across the road, and the people, closer, walking along the footpath, a woman with two kids crossing the road, a postman scooting past on his scooter—he knew that he was done with the doctor. There was nothing left for him in this office. He stood up.

'I'm going now, Dr Feldman.'

'Oh. OK.' The doctor looked at the clock. 'We still have another fifteen minutes of the session to go.'

'I think I'm done.'

'Done?'

'With the sessions.'

Dr Feldman looked over his glasses at Walter, as if this view, unfiltered by ground prescription glass, would give him a different perspective.

'OK,' he said simply.

That was it? That was Dr Feldman's big line, his final pronouncement? No wise words of wisdom, no final diagnosis, nothing for Walter to take away and think about, no affirmation that he was cured, not even a pithy, wry little quote—nothing but a disinterested couple of letters. *Typical.*

On his way out, with his hand on the door handle, Walter turned back for a moment and had his last ever glimpse of Dr Feldman. There he was, standing at his desk, his arm outstretched with a finger pointing to something on the desktop, presumably something he was reading—his appointment book perhaps, or the file of the next patient waiting to see him? A big, rumpled bear of a man in his oversized fleece-lined hoodie. Walter recognised the logo on the hoodie as the Stanford University logo. He was struck by the feeling that this was somehow wrong, a detail that irritated with a sense of being unreal or unconvincing, a cliché from an American movie. He felt suddenly as if, in the act of walking out of this office and closing the door, he would cause Dr Feldman to cease to exist, as if the doctor had only ever existed in his mind in the first place and the sessions had only ever been figments of his imagination. After all, could there really be a psychiatrist quite so cliché as Dr Feldman, with his Stanford University hoodie, his straggling beard, his glasses which he looked over not through—a psychiatrist who actually said: 'Tell me about that'? Was it possible that Dr Feldman was only a …

'Was there something else?'

Walter flinched. For a figment of his imagination Dr Feldman could certainly make him jump.

He closed the door gently.

*

Standing on the street a little later Walter felt drained, completely drained and empty, but at the same time fresh and new and ready to be filled up with something else. In that moment of emptiness everything, every single thing seemed possible to him. The world was filled with promise. That's what he saw in the shop windows and the faces of the passers-by, what he sniffed in the breeze—the just-baked-bread, percolating-coffee, freshly-ironed-shirt, new-car smell of potential. He gave a big sniff of air in through his nostrils, and he had a good, big Polish nose so he got a good lungful.

There were two types of people, Walter had read somewhere—those who when they walked looked up at what was around them, and those who walked along looking at the ground in front of them. Of course Walter was usually in the second category, watching for uneven surfaces, potholes, puddles and dog poo, but that day, after what turned out to be his last appointment with Dr Feldman, wasn't a day to watch the ground in front of him. That day was a day to look up, look out, be alert, because something was out there. Something. Or someone.

Come and get me, he thought, with a rush. *Come and get me.*

15.
DON'T TRUST YOUR WIFE

Walter drove in to Equity after his appointment with Dr Feldman, but he had no intention of settling down to any work. Dev was on his back a bit when he first got in, and insisted he submit the hours he had been away as annual leave. Walter smiled at him and nodded, then booted up his computer but didn't bother logging in.. Instead, as soon as Dev disappeared behind the partition, he pottered around the office, walking with his usual bouncy gait up and down between the open plan workspaces, saying 'Hi' to some of his workmates, nodding to others if they were on the phone, doing little mimes that meant: 'I'll come back.' Everyone seemed slightly surprised that Walter was doing this meet-and-greet round of the floor. He even went out to the Reception desk and leaned on it, waiting until Ros-at-Reception was free. She pressed a button on her phone to transfer the call she was on then looked at Walter with a slight, ever so slight, almost not there, smile on her face.

'Any messages?' he asked.

'No,' she told him, then held up her finger to silence him as she pressed a button on her phone and answered another call.

'Equity-Insurance-good-morning.'

Walter hung around for a second, but the call seemed to be taking a long time so he left and pottered over to the kitchenette. Only one person was there—Mick, who was just flinging a teabag into the bin.

'Hi,' Walter said, leaning back against the cupboard.

'Hey Walter,' Mick said, friendly enough, but as usual giving the impression of not really caring in the slightest.

'What's up?' Walter asked stiffly.

Mick looked at him suspiciously.

'Nothin' much, mate.' He spooned sugar into his tea and stirred. 'The usual shit. What about you?'

'Nothin' much,' Walter echoed.

Mick put the teaspoon on the sink with a clink—he didn't rinse it or put it in the dishwasher, Walter noticed—and walked off without another word. Walter remained leaning against the cupboard. He crossed his arms and his eyes went to the windows, a long way away from the kitchenette and a long way from his own work station. The sky was grey—that was all he could see from this high up. He dropped his arms to his side and walked purposefully back to his desk. He felt itchy, antsy, reckless, as if he'd forgotten his pyjamas and had two cans of gin and tonic all over again. He pocketed his wallet and his new mobile phone, left his briefcase at his desk and, being careful that no-one, especially not Dev, saw him going, he sidled into the foyer and pressed the lift-call button.

Soon he was down on the street, and there on the steps, on the streets, he was gloriously surrounded by them—strangers, hundreds of them. Men and women dressed in their corporate uniform, rushing around him, some talking on mobile phones or earpieces, carrying briefcases, laptops, all on the move, somewhere to be. He stood his ground and allowed himself to be turned around by them, around and around like a turnstile as they passed, hundreds of strangers, and one of them, maybe, would have something to say to him.

He caught the eye of a man approaching him and said: 'Hi' to him. The man nodded in a friendly but distracted manner and kept walking. He said: 'Hello' to another woman and a couple more men. They all acknowledged him, but did not stop to talk. He felt like one of those backpackers employed to stop people on the street and get subscriptions for some charity or other. Perhaps he should use some of their tactics, he thought? The extended hand and the 'My name's Walter, what's yours?' Get one of these strangers to take his hand, return his greeting, *invest in a conversation*? He smiled at the idea, then gave himself up to the pull of the crowd and allowed himself to be swept along the footpath. Usually he was head down, blinkered, busy, on the way somewhere, to work or to the station, but now that he took the time to notice, it was quite exhilarating giving himself up to the flow of the crowd.

Less than half a block away his new mobile phone rang and it took him a moment to realise the unfamiliar ring tone was his. He fumbled it out of his pocket and answered. It was Dev.

'Walter?'

'Dev! I'm so glad you called,' Walter said.

'Where are you Walter?' Dev's voice came through snippy and short. And then, with a sense of outrage that Walter found hilarious: '*Are you outside*?'

'I am, actually, yeah. In fact, at the moment I'm just at the corner of fuck-you and go-get-fucked. Back soon, mate. Bye.'

He hung up and smirked to himself. He never called people mate.

He continued through the city, block by block, carried by the crowd of pedestrians. His phone rang again but he ignored it. He came to a stop at a major intersection and stood amongst all the people streaming past, one after the other, alongside him, past him and across the road. There were so many of them, a different face every couple of seconds or so. So many faces, so many street corners.

It occurred to him then—*how did he know he was on the right street corner?*

How odd, he thought, that it was just as hard to find them as it was to avoid them.

The lights changed and pedestrians crowded past him to cross the road in the other direction. He began to follow them, but stopped, hesitated, drew back. He had thought out of the blue about the bus that had almost run him down. Of course there was no bus there right then and the pedestrians were crossing the road unharmed and un-alarmed, but even so he stepped back from the edge of the road.

What did he think was going to happen to him? Did he think a bus was going to come bearing down on him every time he stepped off a gutter? That was ridiculous. He'd already crossed the street countless times that day. But it didn't have to be a bus, did it? It could be anything really, anything. People died every day in so many different ways, as he knew only too well, knew exactly, precisely, from the little book of his that was at the moment locked away in his suitcase in the boot of his car. He found himself turning around on the spot, watching the pedestrians walk towards him and away from him. There could be no way to tell from which direction it was coming, it came from so many, or when, because it came at any time, and it came to everyone, sometimes out of a clear sky.

He looked up, and that's when he felt it—a hand on his arm, spinning him, literally spinning him, as if someone was whirling him around, deliberately disorienting him. And lips, he felt lips near his left ear, and heard a whisper, more of a hiss really, loud enough to be heard, so close on his ear that he could feel the man's breath, because it was a man's voice that said it.

Don't trust your wife.

Then the hand was gone.

He stopped dead and rocked, slightly off balance. He looked from side to side, all around him, but there was no way to tell who had whispered that warning to him. Pedestrians no longer passed close by him, they didn't spin him around like a turnstile any longer—they were in fact giving him a wide berth, eyeing him suspiciously, hurrying past.

Don't trust Maggie? That was it?

It occurred to him that as a warning it was kind of redundant—he hadn't actually much trusted Maggie ever since she had admitted to infidelity just over a year ago.

*

Walter drove home that night, home that is to Wintergardens rather than to the Pink Flamingo Motor-Inn. He exited the freeway early and picked his way through the surrounding suburbs, taking the back way, for no reason other than to delay getting home.

He found it quite spooky really, driving through those new suburbs on the very edge of the city. There were so many streets and crescents, all with new houses shoulder to shoulder, that they seemed maze-like, and if he at any time took a wrong turn and became disoriented, he could drive around for some time, never quite sure whether or not he had been down any particular street already.

He remembered once arriving at a T-intersection amid this tangle of crescents to find himself unexpectedly on the outskirts of Wintergardens, at the very edge of Melbourne. On the other side of the intersection had been an old fence, a farm fence with wooden posts, weathered and grey, with five rungs of wire, the top barbed wire, all of them rusted and slack, and beyond that nothing but a paddock, flat and dull, with patchy dried grass stretching to the horizon.

That night, driving home the back way, Walter remembered that particular T-intersection and thought suddenly that the world must be flat, because that paddock was undoubtedly the edge. He lived in a flat world, right at the very edge of it, a flat world in which there existed guardian angels.

He felt a sudden urge to find that intersection, if he could, park the car, cross the road, climb through the old barbed wire fence and walk across that old paddock.

He would do it.

It took him a while, but eventually he found the place. He pulled the car up to the T-intersection, but found things different to how he remembered them. There was a billboard directly in front of him with a man and woman holding a toddler-aged child, laughing at something that had apparently happened just prior to the photo being taken. In the background there was a sunset or sunrise, and the suggestion of trees and landscaping. Beyond the billboard the paddock was in the process of being dug up, with piles of earth and heavy machinery standing around, yellow and black and as huge as double-storey houses. The crescents were spreading. The billboard read: NEW COMMUNITY, COMING SOON.

Is that what they were selling, Walter wondered? Community? Electricity and sewers, new streets and streetlights and houses and amenities, yes, but community? Surely you couldn't produce that on cue, you couldn't advertise it and advise it was *coming soon*, a ready-made shake-and-bake community, shiny bright and new, and ready to buy off-the-plan? But obviously he was wrong and community was, these days, in these circumstances, a deliverable on a project plan.

That billboard, Walter thought as he indicated and turned right through the intersection—if he was twenty or so years younger he would spray some obscenity on it.

Of course he would never have done any such thing twenty years ago.

*

When he got home Maggie was in the kitchen preparing dinner. She was chopping vegetables for a dish that was already half prepared and on the stove.

'Hello,' Walter said, appearing in the doorway. 'I'm back.'

She didn't look up from her chopping.

'So I see,' she said.

They said nothing further until dinner, which wasn't surprising to Walter. This was the usual pattern—time apart after a misunderstanding or a stilted, fizzled argument, then sweep it under the carpet, pretend it never happened.

'How was your day?' Walter asked. 'I … ah … I called you, about two. There was no answer.'

'I was out in the garden for a while … maybe it was then … I didn't hear the phone.' Maggie's eyes remained on her dinner plate and she ate another mouthful.

Out in the garden, was she? OK.

Maggie's knife scraped her plate.

'What did you want?' she asked.

'Hmm?'

'Why did you call?'

'Oh, nothing.'

More silence and somewhere in the house the ticking of a clock.

This was silly. This was ridiculous. They had been married for years and there they were sitting in the dining room in uncomfortable, straight-backed, vegetable-eating silence, like they hardly knew each other. Could he have known Maggie so long, so intimately, known so many of her quirks, and she his, shared so many of their days, their big moments and their small ones, and yet still feel a million miles away from her like this, from being able to talk openly and honestly to her?

As he watched her eating—and she did it so nicely, held her fork just so—it occurred to him that he didn't really know her, not really. Maggie had said, hadn't she, so often, that she could read him like a book? She could, he agreed, and so he hadn't felt the pressure to explain himself, to unburden himself of all those awkward, unwieldy emotions. Maggie had just known. But he had never known her, not for sure, had never been able to read her. He only knew that she knew him, which he now realised wasn't quite the same thing. Maggie had known for both of them. She was the one who held it together, held him together, held him down.

'You've hardly eaten a thing,' Maggie said. 'Is it OK?'

'Oh, it's fine,' he said automatically. He looked at the food. No, he had hardly eaten anything. Those carrots, they tasted slightly metallic, didn't they, like the pan they had been cooked in?

'I'm not hungry,' he lied.

And then, out of the blue, with the air of jumping in the deep end, Maggie asked: 'Are you OK, Walter?'

'Fine,' Walter said. 'I'm fine.'

He was surprised to find that he was actually telling the truth. He was feeling OK. In fact he began to feel a familiar uplift, even with Maggie right there in the room, watching on, looking at him suspiciously, with her cutlery balanced elegantly in her fingers. He almost felt the need to grip the edge of the table to keep himself grounded.

*

That night, perhaps unsurprisingly, Walter was unable to get to sleep. Maggie lay beside him, messy and balled up, completely hidden under the sheets and doona. Walter lay tucked up with his head turned towards her. He could see her hair on the pillow and the shape of her shoulder, he could feel her warmth, smell her smell, and hear her breathing. She was asleep—presumably.

Walter carefully lifted the bedding and swung his legs out of the bed. He then inched off the mattress and crept out of the room. He pulled a blanket and a pillow out of the linen cupboard in the hall on the way past and went through into the lounge. There he set up a bed on the couch and climbed in. He knew he wouldn't get to sleep in the bed with her, and if she woke up and noticed he was gone, she'd just think he'd had the dream again and had moved to the spare room to avoid disturbing her. Eventually, at about 3.00am he went to sleep.

*

The next morning Walter left the house as usual, buttoned up and tidy and on time, like clockwork. There was no outward sign of the leak that had begun at Dr Feldman's office the previous day, the feeling of lightness, of floating away, the punchy, light-headed come-and-get-me feeling, nor of the feeling of distance and suspicion that had grown between him and his wife since yesterday, or to be more exact, had been there for some time now. There was no indication, either, that he was not, in fact, that morning, actually going to work. It looked like he was. He was dressed for work in a charcoal suit, white shirt and tie. He carried his briefcase and picked up the home-delivered newspaper, but he wasn't going to work.

He would have to go in sooner or later, he supposed, but in that case why not later? He wasn't relishing the conversation that would have to happen with Dev after his various recent escapades—the days off, the unexplained absences from the office, that meeting where he zoned out, culminating in his profanities to Dev over the phone the previous day. He laughed a little snort of laughter, then bit his lip and pulled a serious face, frowning and holding his lips tight. He couldn't, he knew, not yet anyway, discuss that particular phone-call without smirking, and if he smirked that would only make things worse.

But what did it matter if things were any worse? He was so far gone down that particular slippery slope that he didn't feel there was any way to pull up. Anyway, he didn't particularly want to pull up, or go back, or retract what he had said. Walter wasn't sure, right at that moment, leaving the house, pretending to go to work, that he wanted to go in to the office, not just this morning, but ever again. Not like this, not to the mess that he had created there over the last week or so. They hadn't exactly been his biggest fans in the first place—now he was sure Dev was licking his lips and rubbing his hands together at the prospect of getting rid of him. Walter foresaw meetings with Dev, with HR, various written apologies and perhaps even a written warning for him, the first of three that would result in his termination as an employee of Equity Insurance. In the meantime, of course, while they were waiting for reasons to write the other two written warnings, there would be ongoing performance management and all the bullshit that came with that. In short, he saw the official manoeuvrings of being slowly edged out of the workplace unfolding in front of him like a long winter, and he just didn't have the heart to face the paperwork of it all. Really, he thought, if they wanted to fire him, they should just be allowed to do it—by SMS if they wanted.

If he could go back to how it was, could go back and be the Walter that nobody noticed and that officialdom by and large left alone, if he could go back to that, then he might go back, but there was no going back to that. He mourned that fact at the same time as celebrating it.

He had been different yesterday, a different Walter, new-and-improved, and he woke up to find himself different again today. Perhaps he was going to wake up different every day? The difference? He didn't know what it was, the name of it, all he knew was that the easy things, the default things, the stuff he did every day, at the same tick of the clock, because he'd done it before and knew the outcome and knew it was safe, time after time after time, those things weren't, by and large, an option for him any longer. Certainly not that day. That day he was going to do something ridiculous, something quite possibly dangerous, something no doubt stupid, and he was going to do it willingly.

He walked off towards the train station, still pretending to go to work, with his briefcase in his left hand and the newspaper under his left arm, leaving his right arm and hand free, which, being right-handed, made it easier, just a millisecond or two, but still faster, less muddled, when it came time for him to get his train pass from his right-hand trouser pocket and touch on. He could never understand people who waited until they were right there at the gates of the station, right at the barriers, late for their train, before they looked for their pass, patting their pockets, or rooting around in their handbag frantically. These people always seemed to Walter, as he strode through the barrier almost without breaking stride, the absolute essence of foolishness. It was utterly subconscious, but he thought ahead like this several times a day, and nothing could derail it, because this was Walter, deep down, through and through, dyed in the wool, and Walter, even new-and-improved Walter, was nothing if not a creature of habit.

*

He actually did get on the train that morning, but got off a couple of stops later at Highpoint Shopping Centre where, amongst lots of other things, there was a car rental outlet. There he arranged and paid for a rental car, a light grey Holden with slightly tinted windows. He then drove back to Wintergardens and parked across the street and slightly around the corner from his own house, where, across the lawn of the house on the corner, the Gunderson's lawn, he could see, obliquely, Maggie's little blue runabout in their driveway.

His plan, such as it was, was to follow Maggie and see where she went and who she met. Of course he couldn't use their own car for this in case she looked in the rear-view mirror and recognised it. Perhaps it was a stupid plan—actually, scratch that, obviously it was a stupid plan. If Maggie found out what he was doing she would be livid. It would be more than just another night at the Pink Flamingo Motor-Inn, it would probably be something a lot more permanent. But he wanted to know if she was up to anything, he needed to see for himself. It was the knowing that was important to him.

It had never been the actual infidelity that it hurt him to contemplate, not the nuts and bolts of it, not the sex they must have had. That, in a way, was academic. That, at least, was private and hidden behind closed doors, and he was prudish enough not to want to consider that aspect too closely. What hurt most was the slight, not to his pride or his manhood, he had very little overt pride or masculinity in him, but the slight to his intelligence. It hurt him bitterly to feel so foolish, to feel he was so gullible—the sheer embarrassment of being the cuckolded husband.

He had imagined himself going off to work in the morning, leaving the house and picking up the newspaper and setting off for the train station, perhaps thinking about something stupid like how many steps it took and wondering if it was the same every day, looking at the sky and thinking about what the weather was going to be like, with not a clue in the wide world what was going on behind his back. Literally behind his back. Was Maggie watching him leave? Did she stand at one of the front windows hidden by the curtains, watching until he was out of sight down the road? Did she wait, perhaps, for a couple of minutes longer after he disappeared, to make sure he was well away and definitely not lingering, not coming back for some forgotten article? And what did she do then? Ring this other man? Organise to meet up with him? And did she say when he picked up the phone, *It's OK, he's gone*?

When Maggie had told him about it, had admitted it, he had gone of his own accord to the Pink Flamingo Motor-Inn for a couple of nights, a couple of nights of tossing and turning and fuming, imagining all sorts of conspiracies, all the plotting against him that must have gone on, the withering jibes they might have come out with, or the pity they might have expressed.

Poor Walter.

He hasn't got a clue.

The fool.

At the time, the thought of them conspiring together like this had angered him more than anything, but he had not taken his anger out on Maggie. He did not want to hurt her, even though she had hurt him. He loved her, he supposed—admittedly in what had become an abstract kind of way, even then. Also she was a woman, and you just didn't hurt women, you didn't shout at them and you certainly didn't raise a hand to them.

So he and Maggie hadn't argued about her infidelity at the time, hadn't even, really, discussed it in much depth. Walter had said he would forgive her, had actually said he was prepared to overlook it, of all the pompous things he could have said. He blushed when he thought about it these days. There had been a lot of talk about it never ever happening again, lots of promises and then an agreement, pressed by Walter, that above all they never speak of it.

At the time Maggie had seemed relieved, had seemed, certainly, thankful for Walter's stoic, stiff-upper-lip way of dealing with the situation. But in the last few weeks, months perhaps, it was as if she was wanting to re-visit the whole issue, all this time later. Women, Walter knew from his very limited experience, often wanted to get things out in the open, have things out, dig things up again and have a good old look at them from all angles. He didn't, personally, understand it, but the fact remained Maggie was spoiling for a fight.

What do you think I've been doing, Walter? You and your dirty little mind?

As if she was challenging him to say something, to call her on her behaviour. But why bring it all up again now, a year afterwards?

A figure appeared on the lawn between Walter and his own house. It was Mrs Gunderson with her lapdogs, two explosions of beige and brown fur with no discernible snouts or limbs. One of them she carried. It appeared to have a bandage on one of its legs.

The other wove in and out between her feet, which no doubt explained the injury to the one being carried.

Walter squiggled down in his seat and leaned as far into the back of it as he could, where he hoped he would be invisible from his prying over-the-road neighbour.

Unexpectedly, but of course it was always unexpected, he had another flashback, another flash of memory unlocked from that blacked out portion of his mind, just like the time he remembering the woman doing a Sudoku puzzle, or Missy's husband reading the newspaper. Perhaps it was the sound of the yapping dogs that did it, or being in a parked car, observing from afar—whatever it was, he suddenly thought: *I've done this before.*

He remembered dogs, dogs locked in a car, a big Range Rover type car, with the windows left down a few centimetres. He had been near the car, walking past it or something, and they had been invisible and silent in the interior until he was right up alongside—only then did they begin barking furiously. Yapping little dogs, bouncing up and down on the seats, jumping at the cracks in the window which were smeared with their snotty little nose prints. He remembered it clearly, remembered slapping his hand to his heart and swearing under his breath.

The memory expanded until there was context, and he knew that he had been in a multi-level car park, but not the one near the office where he parked on the occasions he drove to work—this was a different one, in the city, he knew that, but otherwise it was unfamiliar. There was another car nearby—Maggie's car, her little blue run-about. The motor was still clicking, the bonnet was still warm. He remembered feeling it, remembered the warmth under his hand.

The memory expanded further, swamped him like a tide, and he knew why he was there. He had followed Maggie into the city, to this car park.

A rapping sound brought him back to his surrounds with a jolt.

Mrs Gunderson was tapping on the window.

'Walter. What are you doing, love?'

The dog under her arm with the bandaged leg showed its needle-like teeth, fixed him with too-wide eyes and started yapping madly.

He pressed a button on the arm of the car and the driver's side window buzzed down slowly. The yapping became louder.

'Hi, Mrs Gunderson. Sorry. Just fell asleep in the sun for a second there.'

'Have you got a new car?' She was peering into it.

'Nope. Rental. Gotta be going.'

He started up the car and inched away from the curb, buzzing the window up and smiling falsely at Mrs Gunderson.

He drove past his own house and noticed the driveway was empty. The little blue car was gone. Damn. He hadn't even officially started following her before he'd lost her. So typical. He couldn't even do something as simple as follow his wife without stuffing it up.

Walter picked up his mobile, dialled Maggie's number and listened to it ring out.

He felt sure she had heard the ring, sure she had picked up the phone, seen the caller ID, seen that it was him and had ignored it.

Bitch!

16.
AT THE ALBERT HOTEL

Michael Everaardt entered the foyer of the Albert Hotel. It had the reputation of being a little bit daggy, but not in a post-modern, ironic way that could be considered at all cool. He had seen it of course, many times, most recently from the car park across the road, but he had never been inside.

His first impression was very definitely one of faded grandeur—very faded. The only thing left these days that could be called remotely grand was the staircase, which was impossibly, unnecessarily broad, with a heavy wooden banister that curved rather gracefully up and off to both the left and right to a gallery that ran around the room like a mezzanine, with passages leading off to rooms. Otherwise, it was just trashy, he thought, with tatty fittings and furnishings and dusty plastic plants. It looked, he thought, a little like an 80s department store.

He crossed the foyer to a small lounge area near Reception and sat down in a cheap, inappropriately low and soft couch to wait for Maggie. He was amazed that she had agreed to meet him a second time, let alone here at the Albert Hotel. When he had asked her on the phone, only that morning, she had been silent for a moment before quickly rallying.

'Alright,' she had said. Just that one word, but it had sounded to Michael almost as if she was taking up a challenge or a bet. That made him nervous in some way. He wasn't sure he'd like to take a wager against Maggie Kovak.

The previous day, after having visited the multi-level car park, Michael had gone home and read through all the notes and the reports and articles he'd collected about the accident. Eventually he found it—mention of the Albert Hotel. It was in an article about Walter, written without any direct quotes from either Walter or

Maggie, without their input at all, presumably, given that they did not speak with the press. The article described how Maggie had been out on the day of the accident, had spent the day with a friend, shopping and then having afternoon tea. It mentioned that she had taken afternoon tea at the Albert Café.

Michael looked up at the Albert Café. It was located on the mezzanine gallery that travelled around the large foyer, above the entrance to the hotel, with tall arched windows looking down into the street. It was a good spot for a café, but he could tell even from this distance that it would not be a good café. Not, in other words, the sort of place that smart-as-paint Fitzroy-boutique Maggie Kovak was likely to visit for an afternoon tea.

Michael knew, none better, that these sorts of details in these sorts of Sunday-magazine articles were often incorrect—well, perhaps that was a bit rough, perhaps it was best to put it that, like Wikipedia, you wouldn't want to use them as a definitive source—but in this case Michael got the feeling that it was absolutely spot-on. Why would the writer specify the café unless she had somehow got hold of a little bit of accurate information to add colour to the story. It would have seemed an irrelevant titbit, unless, like him, you actually knew where Walter's car had been found three days after the accident.

What it actually meant he wasn't sure, but it was all beginning to—not add up, that would be putting too definite an interpretation on it—but it was beginning to come together in some way. Two apparently irrelevant titbits that, due solely to proximity, were possibly connected and perhaps important in some way. Maggie had been at Café Albert with 'a friend' the day of the accident, and Walter had driven in and parked across the road on that same day. It didn't take an Einstein to make the jump that he had been following his wife—nor to go one step further and make some assumptions about that 'friend' of Maggie's.

Maggie was late again, but again only by a few minutes, as if she doled them out fairly but scrupulously, timing her slightly late arrival to match some rule of etiquette he didn't understand. The accuracy of her lateness made him feel rough around the edges.

Again she had seen him before he spotted her. In fact she was standing at the end of the couch looking at him. How had she managed to do that? He'd been watching the doors. Well, intermittently, but still watching them. He gave a start, then struggled to get up, but the couch was too soft and too low, and he made an awkward mess of it, with his shirt and jacket riding up. Maggie waited politely.

'Hello again,' she said when he had managed to stand up. She didn't offer her hand this time.

'Would you like a coffee?' Michael asked.

She smiled at him, as if sharing a joke, and said, 'Why not?'

They walked together up those inappropriately grand stairs at the rear of the foyer, then doubled back along the mezzanine gallery to the Albert Café. As Michael had suspected, it was a dire little place. There were café tables and chairs squeezed into the floor space—the tabletops were plastic but printed to look like marble, the chairs made of hard moulded plastic. The tables themselves were bare except for salt and pepper shakers, sugar, napkins in a dispenser, and a menu in a plastic stand. The menu had such things on it as cheesecake and lemon slice, but nothing that actually required cooking or even warming up on premises. There was a Midori ad on the wall and more of those dusty fake plants. The place felt bland and slightly unwelcoming and made Michael think of weak filtered coffee.

He and Maggie chose a table alongside one of the large arched windows, which were the most grand thing about the place. Neither of them were bothered about ordering anything, which was lucky as there were no staff in evidence. Through the window

Michael could see the multi-level car park in which Walter's car had been found.

'It seems you've done your research,' Maggie said, following his gaze.

'And that surprises you?'

'It does if you don't mind me saying so. You don't seem the thorough type.'

Michael found Maggie just as difficult to read as the first time he'd met her, and her curious, wandering, slightly inappropriate gaze just as confronting. There was something new about her, though, on this second meeting—a sense of confidence, of triumph maybe, that he didn't quite understand and didn't much like.

'You know why, don't you?' he asked, jumping in the deep end. 'You know why he drove into town and parked over there.'

'I don't *know*.'

'But you have a pretty good idea.'

She looked at him steadily, looked at his mouth again. Always his mouth. Why?

'I presume he was following me,' she said simply.

'And where were you?'

'As I think you know,' she said. 'I was here.'

'Having coffee with a friend?'

'No,' she said. 'That was a lie. Well, a slight variation on the truth.'

'So where were you then?'

She lifted her eyes to the ceiling.

'Upstairs.'

Michael began to smile.

'Stop smirking,' she said.

'Sorry.'

She shrugged and made a little wiggle of it, which communicated a general sort of discomfort or distaste. At what,

Michael wondered—this whole scene with him, or the memory of what she had done?

'It was a … a local man,' she went on, remarkably frank. 'A neighbour. A married man.'

Michael nodded.

'There's no need to go into details now. It was only brief in any case. It was stupid really, I guess—so close to home. Anyway, it turned out I was just one of a series of women, and I didn't particularly like being just one of many. I hated being such a cliché, quite frankly—bored and horny housewife—but there you go, perhaps we're all a bit more obvious than we like to think?'

She wasn't obvious, Michael thought. She was anything but obvious. She was, what was the word—inscrutable?

'So this was going on just before the accident?'

'Yes.'

'And Walter knew about it?'

'Oh yes. He won't talk about it, though.'

'Won't talk about it?'

'Refuses to discuss it.'

'He knew about it though. At the time, I mean.'

'He found out, yes.'

'And you think he was following you that afternoon?'

She shrugged again.

'Why else would he be there, right across the road?"

'Does he remember it? Following you here? Parking over there?'

'No,' she said, and she smiled as if this amused her, but then her smile faded. 'Well …' she said and stopped.

Michael waited.

'He says he doesn't,' she continued. 'But I wonder sometimes whether he's telling the truth about what he does and doesn't remember?'

'You think he might remember more than he's letting on?'

'It would be a good excuse, wouldn't it? For someone like Walter who doesn't ... admit to things, doesn't want to face unpleasant truths, shies away from conflict. It would be a good excuse,' she repeated.

Michael stared at her, but his mind suddenly raced on elsewhere. So Walter followed his wife in to town that day, was spying on her as she went for a tryst in this shabby, forgotten city hotel. Did he want to find out for sure what was going on? Did he want to know who she was going to meet? A neighbour Maggie had said. Did he know who the man was? Did he only suspect? Or did he follow her here in the hope of finding out? And then what?

I want to know what happens next, Michael thought.

Maggie was smiling at him, he realised, a little smile of triumph.

'I've told you all this,' she said, 'quite openly.'

'Yes,' he said carefully, feeling his way.

'But I don't quite see what business it is of yours.' She smiled at him. 'I also don't quite see what you intend to do with the information. It can't possibly be of any use to you, can it? Not really? Not for the sort of article you want to write.'

She was looking at him again, one of those frank, too-intimate looks that took in his eyes and nose and his lips, the tuft of hair under his bottom lip, his chin, his throat and perhaps even down to the thumb indent in his collar bone, where a little hair from his chest curled over the top of his t-shirt.

'I have a room,' she said evenly.

'What?' he said. He had heard her, of course, but it was such an about-face that his response was automatic.

'I have a room,' she said again. 'Upstairs.'

'Here?'

'It is a hotel.'

He wasn't disputing the fact that you could in fact book rooms at the Albert, he was just taking a while to catch up, that's all. It had been like that all along, he realised, with him struggling to keep up with her pace, her abrupt changes of conversation, lagging behind a step or two.

'You know,' Maggie went on. 'Ever since we met I've been wondering what that little bit of hair, just there,' she pointed to the tuft of hair underneath his lower lip, 'would feel like.'

He knew what she meant and for a second he allowed himself to consider it—couldn't help it. In a flash he imagined the pale, smooth skin on her inner thighs and imagined how it would feel under his hands, against his cheeks. He imagined his tongue inside her, lapping at her. A moment longer and he would be able to taste it, to smell it.

So he got up and followed her—of course he did—and as he did he felt foolish for being so easily lead, as surely as if he had a Prince Albert with a leash clipped on it, but he only felt it for a moment, because he was young enough not to be unduly upset about following his cock. He watched Maggie's arse as he followed her to her room in the Albert Hotel, and his dick began to stiffen.

*

Having failed in the simple task of tailing his wife, Walter returned the rental car. He negotiated with quiet dignity, but was unable to convince them to give him a refund, or even a part refund.

Arseholes. He'd only had the fricken thing for just over an hour!

He looked at his watch. It was only mid morning and he didn't have a lot of options for the rest of the day. He had no intention of going in to work to face the music there, and couldn't go home in case Maggie showed up unexpectedly. There was nothing much else to do but spend the rest of the day at Highpoint. He went through shop after shop, at first with purpose, but soon with a slouch and a wary eye, mooching around and on edge in case someone saw him.

He browsed into an army disposals store and walked listlessly along aisles of camping equipment, tents and sleeping bags, freeze-dried foodstuffs and various bits and pieces of survival gear. He had no idea what most of it was. He picked up some kind of pump and turned it this way and that. It looked kind of like a bicycle pump, but different. It had a long snout and a dingle thing hanging off the end. He gave it a few experimental pumps and it expanded in an unexpected way that made him jump.

'Walter. Hi.'

He spun around. It was Missy. The pump in his hand wheezed and deflated in an obscene and comic way. He jammed it back on the shelf.

Missy looked just as fresh and lovely as ever, with her sports shoes and her leggings and her little cardigan and her messy hair held at the back of her head in a hinged-comb. She had her two girls with her this time, with their black eyelashes and hair, the colouring inherited from their father. At first they hung onto her, but soon they moved around vaguely, exploring their surroundings, forcing the distance-from-Mum wider and wider until the time came to be called back in. Missy had obviously been shopping as she carried bags of things, Walter wasn't sure what, netting and sparkling things, and a lot of pink.

'Costumes for the girls,' she said, noticing him looking. 'They've got a party next weekend. One wants to go as a Disney Princess,' she rolled her eyes. 'The other wants to go as a sushi roll.'

'A sushi roll?'

'Don't ask me.' She shrugged.

Missy smiled and nodded at Walter in a way that said, 'We've got two minutes until they rip this place apart, so let's get on with it.'

'Not at work today?' she asked.

'No. Day off. Bit of shopping.'

'You going camping or something?'

'No. No, probably not.'

She nodded as if that made absolute sense and looked over his shoulder to check on the girls.

'Daisy, don't touch that.'

Daisy—a cute name for a little girl. Walter wondered if she was the Disney Princess or the sushi roll. Missy and Daisy and …

'What's your other daughter's name?'

'Margaret, after my mother. She's the oldest. We call her Peg.'

Missy and Daisy and Peg. It sounded like they should be characters in a children's story. No husband, though, just the girls these days. Walter wondered if she would bring it up, the absent husband, but she didn't appear to be in the same mood as the other day at the NGV, not as watchful, not as hopeful, probably because the girls were there. Her eyes kept slipping past him, keeping an eye on them. The other day at the gallery it had been, for just a stolen hour or so, not about the girls but about her.

'Can I ask you something?' Walter said out of the blue.

'Sure. What?' She looked at him innocently.

'Do you believe in a higher power? That there's something out there? Something that's … I don't know … watching over us?'

She blinked at him a couple of times and her face was blank. He thought she was going to give some glib, dismissive answer, or simply ignore his question completely, but she did not. After a second or two she said slowly:

'I don't know … but …'

She stopped and met his eye, a little embarrassed.

'But what?' Walter prompted.

'If I tell you about this do you promise you won't laugh?'

'I wouldn't laugh.'

'Well, it's just that for the last year or so I've been finding an awful lot of five cent coins.'

'Five cent coins?'

'Yes. On the street, you know. Just walking along.'

Walter nodded.

'Yes, and …'

'And nothing. That's it. I mean, I've never really thought about five cent coins. Have you?'

Walter shook his head. Missy continued:

'No, you don't. But like I said, I've just started noticing that lately I'm seeing so many of them … and it's got to the point that it's too much of a coincidence … it feels different … it feels as if … I don't know … as if the universe is telling me something.'

'The universe?'

She shrugged.

'The universe—yes.'

'Telling you something like … ?'

'I don't know. But it feels positive. As though it's a sign that I'm travelling in the right direction, that everything's going to be OK. That's all.'

'All out of a couple of five cent coins?'

She made a face at him with a mock frown.

'You're laughing at me and you said you wouldn't.'

'Oh, I'm not … I'm not laughing at you. I'm … I … So who do you think is doing it?'

'Doing what?'

'Putting those five cent coins in your path?'

'I don't think anyone's doing it.'

'Well you must believe something is making it happen.'

She looked puzzled for a second.

'No … no I don't. It's not something I believe in, as such, it's just … something I feel.'

Walter gaped at her, but at that moment her attention was diverted to her daughters.

'Daisy, don't touch that,' she said again.

'You're very lucky,' he told her. She had said the exact same thing to him, he remembered, the last time they'd met. 'They're lovely girls. And you …' he swallowed, felt his Adam's apple jump around in his throat, then took his courage in his hands, right there in the Army Disposals Store. 'You are very beautiful.'

He had never, never ever told a woman that she was beautiful ever before in his life, not even Maggie. He felt exhilarated and, again, quite reckless. He wondered if this was how it felt to be unfaithful. The idea did not displease him—him, Walter Kovak, unfaithful.

For a second Missy seemed surprised by the compliment. Her eyes dropped and she looked as if she was trying to smother a smile. It was charming, he thought, she was charming, to be so pink-cheeked and modest about being offered a compliment like that. Accept it, he thought, enjoy it, smile at it.

'I'm so sorry,' Walter said.

She looked up at him, puzzled.

'For what?'

But he couldn't say what he was sorry for. He could barely articulate it to himself. His thoughts were a muddle and he'd just blurted it out without thinking. He felt, in a way, without fully understanding, a sense of responsibility for Missy. Why? Because she was widowed and left to cope alone with her one wage, two little girls and a mortgage on a house in Wintergardens? Because she was a woman, and he felt some sort of cave-man style tug right down inside him that made him want to protect her? Because her husband had been regularly unfaithful to her and her memory of him would be forever tainted by his infidelities? Because she would never get the chance now he was dead to move beyond that, to slap him, throw something at him, kick him out—or if she felt inclined a different way, to forgive him. *You can't slap the dead*, Walter thought—well, not once they're buried. You're stuck with them then, stuck with whatever they were at the moment they died. You could forgive them though, he thought after a moment. He remembered the way Missy had showed him the photo of Aristo in her purse that day at the NGV, remembered her face when she asked if he could recall any of her husband's last moments in the train. He knew that she had forgiven him. How odd, Walter thought, that she should be so forgiving. Odd and wonderful.

Suddenly he knew his *I'm sorry* was totally inadequate.

There was a clang and rumble from deep in the shop as of various carefully piled up things falling to the floor. Their few minutes were up it seemed. Missy's attention turned from him. The moment was gone and Walter's shoulders slumped.

'Girls! Get out here. Come on, we're going. Come on. Now.'

The girls emerged and grabbed onto the straps of the shopping bag obediently, obviously knowing the drill. When they were anchored and Missy was ready to move off, she paused for a second and looked back at Walter.

'Thanks,' she said, in a more matter-of-fact tone. 'Really. You're a very kind man.'

There was something in the way she said it, Walter felt, that was sad, or apologetic maybe. He didn't quite understand that, not when he was the one who was sorry.

*

The upstairs passageways at the Albert Hotel were wide and generous, the ceilings high, the walls thick, and the doorways large, but the room itself, when Michael and Maggie got to it, was narrow and awkwardly shaped, although perhaps it seemed smaller than it was due to the height of the ceiling. The ornate plasterwork of the cornice was incongruous alongside the quality of furniture and fittings—not cheap exactly, but hardly luxurious. The beds were slightly squat, the covers and pillows flat. Everything was done in a colour scheme of beige, a biscuity-brown and mauve. The room was adequate without being in any way welcoming or enjoyable.

They fucked on the squat bed. It had been rather no-holds-barred and Michael had felt a mix of abandon and concern that they might be heard in the next room. Not that he had seen a single other person along the corridor on their way upstairs. No wonder Maggie liked this place for her nooners, he thought—it was totally deserted.

And now it was all over. He'd come inside her. She'd gone to the bathroom very briefly, and now she was at the end of the bed getting dressed. That was that, it seemed. Done and dusted. Michael, still naked, lay in bed covered with a sheet, watching her. Had he been at home he would have lit a cigarette, but he eyed the smoke detector way up on that high ceiling warily. He wouldn't like to chance it. Not in the circumstances.

She wore stockings, he noticed—none of the girls of his own age that he'd slept with wore stockings—and at that moment he felt the difference in age between himself and Maggie acutely. Minutes ago he'd been inside her, now he felt a millions miles away from her.

'What are you?' he said.

'I beg your pardon?'

'What are you?'

'That sounds like it's meant to be rude.'

'It's not. I just don't get you. What are you? A femme fatale? Or a desperate housewife?'

'You're so young,' she said dismissively.

'That's not an answer.'

'What was the question?'

'Who are you? Really?'

She stepped into her skirt and pulled it up.

'You think I know?'

'I thought you might.'

She shook her head and zipped up her skirt.

'I have to get home,' she said.

As she finished getting dressed—or finished putting herself back together as Michael phrased it to himself—he thought about that home and he wondered if she and Walter had ever been happy.

'Why don't you leave?' he asked, following out his own train of thought.

'You mean him? Why don't I leave him?'

He nodded.

'Yes. Why don't you leave him?'

She stopped, her shoes in her hand, and looked at the wall above his head as if lost in thought. That's when he saw it, just for a second—a big yawning ache inside her, as if for something lost or something promised but never attained. It was only for a second though, and after that second she bent down and put her shoes on. When she stood up she spoke, but it wasn't, at least not immediately, an answer to his question.

'His name was Aristo. He left me here. We agreed to go back to Wintergardens separately. He went to the train station. I had the car. He was … in the accident also. He died. Walter, I suppose, was following him.'

'Why?'

'I don't know,' she said. 'Because he couldn't help it?' She paused for a second. 'I do know that if it wasn't for me, he wouldn't have been on the train.'

Michael wasn't sure which 'he' she was talking about, but thought it most likely she was thinking of her husband. He swung his legs off the bed, got up and walked naked to the window. He pushed aside the curtain and looked across the road to the car park which looked directly into this room, or would if it weren't for the gauzy curtain. If Walter was across there right now, he would see him, Michael, standing there staring back, pale-chested and slightly unfit but young enough to get away with it.

He would see me, Michael thought, and he felt like an absolute arsehole.

Maggie spoke from behind him and he turned around to find her fully put back together, poised and in control, with her coat over her arm. He had the urge to cover up his cock and balls with his hands, cup them protectively like a soccer player, but fought it. He felt incredibly vulnerable, naked in front of her with his back to the window—as if any second there would be gunfire from the car park across the street, the window would shatter and he would be mown down by a hail of bullets. A stupid thought.

'I have to go,' she said.

'Sure.'

She turned towards the door then turned back again. It was a slightly stagey movement, and he felt sure she'd done it on purpose. He wondered what was coming.

'The article,' she said.

He hadn't expected that. Or, actually, now that he thought about it, perhaps he had expected it. It had a ring of inevitability about it that made it feel expected.

'I don't think we'd like to be involved after all.'

Of course not. He nodded and smiled and felt suddenly like laughing. He felt as if everything that had come before, from the moment he spoke to Maggie on the phone that first time, or before that even, from the moment he saw her get out of that car at the hospital, from the moment he took that photograph of Walter emerging from the wreckage in the dust cloud, everything had been leading to and was completed by this moment. This was the cherry on top—pop, right there. What could he do but laugh? If you didn't laugh, you'd cry.

'Of course not,' he said in a manner he hoped was gallant. He felt magnanimous in defeat—because that's undoubtedly what it was. Maggie, whatever she was or wasn't, and he still had no idea about that, wasn't one to be fucked with. She could be fucked, obviously, but she wasn't one to be fucked with. He felt no animosity about it.

He heard the door latch and he realised that she had slipped out, leaving him there without a further word. Everything seemed a little bit more tatty without her in the room, but in a way he felt comforted by his solitude.

His mind began to wander. He began to think about his article and what he would and wouldn't put in it. He had a sudden urge to begin on it immediately. If only he had his laptop with him, he would have enjoyed propping himself up in the bed—after all the room was bought and paid for until check-out the next day—and writing it right there on the scene of the crime.

No, he wouldn't mention either Walter or Maggie. There were others who had been in the accident and survived, there were other widows and widowers, grieving mothers and sisters and brothers. There were enough people out there who courted notoriety. He would track one or two of them down, give them their fifteen minutes of fame. He would leave Maggie and Walter alone, he thought, with whatever it was that they had left.

17.
WALTER GETS ON THE NEXT TRAIN

Late that afternoon Walter made his way back to the closest train station. He had wasted the entire day wandering around Highpoint. He felt as dried up as a beef jerky from spending so long in the climate controlled environment. He managed to catch the exact same train he would normally be on so that right on his regular time he disembarked at Wintergardens. He walked those few blocks home through the fading light, his briefcase at his side, his steps regular and even. Just like any other normal day.

He reached his own street, walked past the neighbours' houses and was soon out the front of his own house. He was home.

He stood on the footpath at the mouth of the driveway for some time, watching as the house and garden turned just slightly purple in the very last of the twilight.

Home.

Soon he saw Maggie moving around inside, apparently unaware of his presence. She turned on a light in the front room, then, a second or two later, the porch light came on also. At the very same moment the streetlights up and down the street flickered on, as if synchronised. All that electric light emphasised the darkness, and time seemed to rush on somehow, give a sharp jolt, jump forward, and Walter thought suddenly: *I'm not going inside.*

*

He stood right there, right where he was, in the driveway, until he became aware of a strain in his shoulder. He bent and put his briefcase beside his feet then straightened up again and rolled his shoulder once or twice. He had no idea how long he'd been standing there, but it was darker and getting, if not cold, then at least a bit nippy.

Earlier on there had been a couple of passers-by, a woman jogging and an old couple walking briskly. At first Walter had hoped the jogging woman was Missy, feared the walking couple were the man and his wife from the other night, but he hadn't known any of them. There had been no-one for some time.

The longer he stood there, hesitated in the driveway, the longer he delayed going in, the greater was his sense of resolve, of clarity, the more he knew he wouldn't go in.

How ridiculous. What am I doing?

But he didn't feel ridiculous.

*

'What are you doing out here?'

It was Maggie in the darkness beside him.

Walter, now sitting cross-legged in the driveway on a frigid backside, hadn't heard her approach and he jumped slightly at the sound of her voice. She certainly hadn't come out the front door and crossed the front lawn in the light. She must have come up in the darkness from the side of the house somewhere. She moved between him and the porch light and became a silhouette in the darkness, a silhouette with the orange glow of cigarette floating up towards the mouth. How had he missed that glowing cigarette tip in the darkness? She exhaled and the smoke was illuminated by the porch light.

'Walter?' she said when he didn't respond.

'What?'

'Are you OK?'

'I'm fine,' he said automatically. Surely, though, it was patently untrue this time, just another pleasantry, another in the long line of 'Yes Dears' in Walter's life? He was sitting cross-legged in his driveway in the middle of the night with his briefcase beside him and no intention of entering his own house—could he really be, in any sense of the word, fine?

'Has something happened?' Maggie asked.

'Happened?'

'At work today? Did something happen?'

'I didn't go to work today.'

'You didn't?'

'No, I didn't. I'm not sure I'm going to go back there.'

'Did you quit?'

'Not really.'

'Not really? What does that mean?'

Walter didn't answer.

After a moment Maggie dropped her cigarette butt and stepped on it. Walter would normally have objected, of course, but right then he couldn't be bothered.

Then, unexpectedly, Maggie sat down next to him on the cement. She folded her legs carefully, elegantly beneath her.

'Did you see Dr Feldman today?'

He shook his head.

'No. I went yesterday though.'

'What did he say?'

'Nothing much.'

'Did he give you a prescription?'

'Medication? No. why?'

'I just wondered. You seem …'

She paused and he interrupted.

'I'm done with the Doctor.'

'Really?'

He didn't answer.

'Walter what's going on?'

'I don't …'

'Tell me.'

'I don't know.'

'Tell me,' she said again, and her voice sounded different somehow, different in an unexpected way—softer? Walter looked across at her in time to see her bring both of her hands up to her face. She covered her cheeks and eyes and bent her head. She didn't make a sound, but sat like that for some time. When she dropped her hands and turned to him, her face in the porch-light was as vulnerable as Walter had ever seen it. He blinked in the glare of her unexpected vulnerability. Of course he wanted to reach out to her, comfort her. She was close enough to touch, close enough for him to put his arm on her shoulder and make a soothing noise, but he didn't. Something in him hardened, became suspicious.

'You're up to something,' he said.

'What?' Her voice was still softer than usual.

'You must be. They told me.'

She blinked a couple of times.

'They? Told you what?'

'Not to trust you,' Walter said darkly.

Something in her face receded from him as he watched. It was as if she unfolded then re-folded herself in a different shape. Her eyes were suddenly dry and she looked at him steadily.

'Who told you that?'

Walter didn't answer.

'I've never trusted you,' he said in a matter-of-fact voice. 'Not really. Not since you had that affair. I just tried ... not to think about it.'

'Walter, who said this to you?'

Walter ignored her. He felt removed from everything. He got to his feet, stretched out his cramped legs and picked up his briefcase.

'I'm not going inside, you know,' he said. 'I'm not going inside the house.'

*

He walked to the Wintergardens train station. It was so different being there in the night, slightly unreal. It had the harsh over-lit quality of a crime scene or a UFO landing. There was only one other person on the platform, a very skinny young man, a youth, standing directly under a light at the other end of the platform, his hands deep in his pockets. He appeared to be wearing some sort of white jacket, with a hood up, but being directly under the light there was a harsh shadow inside the hood and Walter couldn't see a face at all. He felt a jolt of recognition, not for the man, but for the circumstance.

So that was it. This was the next one, the fifth.

He felt instantly excited, elated even. He took a breath and made an effort to keep it together—but it was too late, really, for keeping it together, wasn't it? What did he have left to keep it together for? Nothing. There was nothing left. He'd walked away from everything—his job, his marriage, his house.

He walked up the platform towards the young man, and as he approached he realised that it wasn't shadow under the hood, it was dark skin, pitch black skin. It was an African man, no more than a young teen, just a kid really. Walter could see the yellow-white of the young man's eyes as he looked at him. There were ipod earphones disappearing into the hood at either side of his head, and as Walter came closer he poiked one of the ipod earpieces out and wrinkled up one side of his lip in a sneer.

'Fuck off,' the black kid said succinctly. His voice was deep.

Walter laughed.

'Oh come on. What is it this time?'

He said nothing.

'Come on. I can hack it. What's the next one? What am I looking out for this time? Cos whatever it is, I'm gunna do it this time. I'm gunna do it.'

The black kid moved his jaw arrogantly, as if chewing something, but said nothing.

'Don't get on the next train?' Walter asked. 'That's a classic, that one.'

'Fuck,' the kid said, articulating very carefully, 'off.'

The kid's eyes slipped away to the side, and Walter turned and looked in the same direction. He saw the glow of a train's approaching lights. He listened for the sound in the darkness, and it came to him, softly, from far away—the *rickety-clack rickety-clack* of his dreams.

He felt himself go rigid with the sudden thought: *How easy would it be to throw myself on the tracks?*

The train, he supposed, would still be travelling with a certain amount of speed as it drew into the station, enough to crush him to bits. Not, his precise mind decided after another second, that there was any necessity for speed as such. He looked at the tracks, silvery in the light, and imagined the wheels of the train moving over them like a blade—even a train inching forward centimetre by centimetre could probably slice his head off.

There was only a moment to decide, but before he could make up his mind either way the train was pulling into the station. It came to a stand-still and the doors opened. Walter stepped towards the carriage, then away. Again he was moving like a praying mantis—his feet firmly planted and his body moving back and forward. He was rubbing his hands together, occasionally wiping his palms on his thighs, or down the side of his pants. He found himself excited but petrified with it.

Don't get on the next train, the man had said all that time ago.

But why not?

There was nothing out here on the platform for him.

Or at home.

Or anywhere else.

So why not get on the train?

At the very last minute Walter stepped into the carriage.

The doors began beeping and closed behind him.

*

There was no-one else in the carriage with Walter.

He was totally alone.

And that felt? Good? Bad?

He didn't know.

The train began moving forward out of the station. Walter saw the black kid through the window. He had put his ipod earpiece back in. His eyes followed Walter as the carriage went past and he put his middle finger up and mouthed two words that it wasn't difficult to lip-read.

Well that, Walter supposed, was that.

He went to the end of the carriage and sat down.

He felt completely empty.

The lights in the carriage flickered, as if there was an interruption to the power for a moment or two. In those flickering moments, Walter became aware of the darkness of the suburb outside, Wintergardens, surrounding him, pressing in on the train carriage. It was only for a moment, though, before the lights came on again and the interior of the carriage, his own face, was reflected in the windows again.

So what now?

As if in answer the lights flickered again and when they came back on he saw, not an empty carriage but a carriage half full of people—regular everyday people, minding their own business. He sucked in his breath as he realised what he was seeing. He tried to block the memory, but found that he couldn't. There they were—the woman beside him doing a Sudoku puzzle, and directly across from him the man reading the newspaper, Missy's husband Aristo.

Walter realised as he saw Aristo in his memory that what he told Missy at the art gallery was wrong. Aristo had not been reading a newspaper, he, Walter, had been reading the newspaper. He understood the memory more clearly now. He saw his own fingers, his own hand holding the newspaper. Yes, he could see Aristo's face over the newspaper, around it, but he, Walter, was the one reading it. No, actually, he wasn't *reading* it, he was holding it up as if he was reading it, but he wasn't. What was that all about?

As had happened with the memory of the car park and the yapping dogs in the car, Walter was suddenly aware of more than just what he was seeing in his memory, he was aware of context. He was hiding behind the newspaper. He was watching Aristo. He was following him.

Walter began to get a strange feeling, a feeling that there was something here he wasn't, after all, prepared for.

He didn't remember the accident as such, had no memory of any impact. He couldn't remember people being thrown down, or anyone crying out or anything actually happening at all. All he remembered was a sudden darkness. In fact he remembered thinking: *Why is it suddenly dark?* It felt foolish to have been so dense at the time.

After the darkness, though, he remembered feeling a gradual awareness of the physical nature of his predicament seeping into him. He realised that, amazingly, he seemed to be balled up as if halfway through a somersault or something, bunched up uncomfortably, jammed against, half under something, his face pressed into his knees. He squirmed around, slowly, tentatively, tensing the muscles in his legs and arms and torso, until he worked out where the various bits of his body were, how exactly he was folded up. Once aware of his body again he felt, instinctively, automatically, that he needed to get up, unfurl and reorient himself, let gravity take hold of him again.

He slowly, carefully unfolded himself backwards until his bum was resting on his heels and from there, quite simply, he sat up in the darkness. With this reorientation other things became apparent—a nasty pull somewhere in his back, pain in his shoulder and hip where he had presumably been thrown down, bile in his throat, dust, it seemed, in his nose, all these things made themselves known, but in general he found he was OK.

From there he began to understand something of what must have happened. No, that wasn't quite right. He had no clear concept of what had happened, but he began to remember where he had been just moments before this dark, muddled mess he was now experiencing. He had been on a train, he knew, and something, he realised, slowly, stupidly, must have happened to the train.

It was at this point that he began to feel the emotion of the situation, a prickle of fear that he felt in his groin and his underarms first before it flowed through him entirely. He felt perspiration bead on every part of him in seconds flat. He had to get out of there immediately.

But how? Where to?

He extended his arms, his fingers waving and wriggling, urgent but tentative, exploring the edges of his new pitch-black world, the space he had to escape from. His fingers explored, found surfaces, metal and stone and rubble, a mixture of different feelings under his fingertips.

With a jerk of horror his arms recoiled to his chest.

He had felt something soft.

He sat silent and still in the darkness, petrified, fiercely concentrating on the place in the darkness where his fingers had felt that softness. He began to believe he was getting an understanding of the space around him, felt sure he could discern deeper shadows within the dark, edges, slight differences in the texture of the darkness, and right in front of him an unexpected patch of paleness.

He became convinced he could hear breathing, someone else breathing alongside him, almost in sync with him so that it was impossible to discern the separate rhythm.

There was someone else there.

It was his dream—the darkness and the knowledge that there was someone else in it with him, someone else unseen but close-by.

He focussed on that paleness until it seemed, dreamlike, to begin to resolve itself into … what? Was it an arm? A shoulder? A face? Yes a face. And as he saw it more clearly, the less scary it became—less scary and also … familiar. It was the man he had been watching from behind the newspaper, the man he had been following. It was the man who had been at that city hotel with Maggie, Missy's husband Aristo.

Walter realised something was wrong with what he was remembering.

Aristo was breathing.

He wasn't dead.

He had been alive after the accident.

Walter had been right, his dreams had been right. There *had* been someone else there with him in the dark. He hadn't been the only one, the sole survivor, after all. But in that case …

Aristo said something then. His voice was weak and uncertain. He didn't have his eyes open, he didn't seem to realise that Walter was even there, kneeling just to the side of him in the gloom. He was just saying it to himself, to no-one in particular. Something about his legs.

Walter turned his head, looked at Aristo's legs, or where his legs should have been. It was instead a mess of debris, the remains of a slab of concrete. He was pinned down and his legs must be a complete mess underneath.

Walter's fear suddenly left him. There was no fear, no foolishness, there was no emotion whatsoever. He bent down to pick up a chunk of the concrete wreckage from Aristo's legs. He remembered how it felt in his hands, that chunk of concrete he picked up, how rough it was, heavier than he expected, more difficult to lift than he thought it would be.

He remembered heaving it up as high as he could in the confined space and slamming it down on Aristo's face.

He remembered killing him.

*

There was another memory, just one more. The light. That was the last thing he remembered, that little sliver of daylight, and he remembered moving towards it, automatically, through the gloom, breathing shallow breaths in the dust, until the sliver of light became a triangle, and then, then something else, some other shape, ragged at the edges but big enough for him to get his head and shoulders through. He remembered pushing through it and rising up and out through the space into the sky.

*

Slowly, blinking a bit, Walter became aware of his actual surroundings again. There were no further disinterred memories to see, only the empty carriage he was sitting in with his own face reflected in the window. There was nothing to feel but the sway of the train, the swing of it, the galloping pace and pulse of it—nothing to hear but the *rickety-clack rickety-clack*. It was just him in a train carriage heading into the city through the outer suburbs, just him, Walter, sitting there, all by himself. Alone. But he wasn't alone, was he? Travelling with him, outside the train, the other side of the window, at his shoulder, streaming along in the night air, was the thing in his dreams, in the gloom, that he had to run away from, the shadow within himself of blacked out memories, unanswered questions, unplumbed depths, that feeling of disquiet, difference, disconnect, the feeling there was more to him, that he didn't fit his own life, that inside him was the potential for something else.

So this was it?

He had killed a man.

He sat with it for a minute.

Then he shook his head.

He expected to feel more.

Shouldn't he feel more? Remorse? Or horror? Something? Instead of this feeling of … what was it? After the blackness … this feeling of … of sheer, blinding-white relief.

It was as if, for the first time in a long time, he was totally lit-up right through, up and down and into every part of him—and every smutty little page of him, every dark corner, every whorl of his guilty fingerprints, every bit, every nerve, every crevice, every part of him was for a change fluorescent-lit for the world to see.

*

Walter got off the train at the North Melbourne station. He felt numb. He thought a little about what he should do next. He felt, instinctively, that he should make a clean breast of it—he was after all a law-abiding citizen. Yes, he would confess, he thought, but in the light of his new-found self-knowledge, he didn't want to do it straight away.

He considered, for a second, making his way back to Wintergardens, out of habit more than anything, but he knew he couldn't. The angels had taken Wintergardens away from him along with everything else, had stripped him totally bare until he had nothing but the knowledge of what he had done. Perhaps that was God's bidding.

No, he needed to start fresh, from right there at North Melbourne station. Take one step at a time. He took one step, then another, and walked towards the exit.

He would seek out a police station, he supposed, or—he remembered being visited by that young man, the scruffy young man with the apologetic look, the journalist. What had his name been? Ever-something. He would find that journalist, perhaps, and tell him the truth about the accident. Perhaps.

He came out of the station and turned up a side street. He would decide soon, he thought, what to do.

He put his hands in his pockets. There were some loose coins in there. He brought them out and looked at them in his hand. Amongst other more substantial coins there was a five cent piece, small and light and totally useless.

He thought of Missy and her girls back in Wintergardens. There, if you like, was something he could walk towards—a different Wintergardens driveway with something else at the end. For a moment he had a vivid flash of how his life could be, could have been—but no, that wasn't possible. He had, after all, killed her husband. You had to be pragmatic about these things.

He picked out the five cent piece from amongst the other coins on his palm, positioned it on his thumbnail and flicked it away into the shadows. He didn't see it land, but he heard it. He would leave it there for her to find.

www.ingramcontent.com/pod-product-compliance
Lightning Source LLC
LaVergne TN
LVHW091137080826
845145LV00008B/2183

* 9 7 8 0 9 8 7 4 0 3 7 0 4 *